Dormant

Rogue Spark

Cameron Coral

Stay updated on Cameron's books by signing up here:
CameronCoral.com/sign-up

You'll be added to my reading list, and as thanks I'll send you a digital copy of *CROSSING THE VOID: A Space Opera Science-Fiction Short Story*

Contents

Chapter 1
Carnival

I run. It's been months—years, maybe? I run along rolling green hills at the ocean's edge, into copper-hued canyons, and through forests.

I'm tired. I run with no destination. "Move," I tell my sore feet.

Because he's chasing me.

Vance. That was his name. My memories are hazy. I know he's evil and will hurt me if he catches me. He hurt people I knew, people I cared about. But I didn't let him kill them. I touched them and brought them back to life. Before he could destroy more people, I stopped him.

———

Darkness surrounds me, and I've been running for a long time. No sign of Vance, so I stop for a rest. I'm in an unkempt field where a scraggly brush reaches my thighs. I pinch the leaves, and they crumble between my fingers. Dead.

Ahead of me, in the distance, I spy objects. A collection of rides and tents and hastily built wooden shacks, and there's a giant big-top tent like in old movies. I search my mind for the word... carnival.

But the shuttered carnival looks run down, weathered by time, and forgotten by the children who once begged their parents to bring them here.

A cutting wind chills my aching body, pushing me on. As I near the entrance, a lonely rusty gate swings back and forth. I scan behind for any sign of Vance. Alone for now, but I'm sure he'll find me soon. He always does.

Decaying smells surround me, discarded memories hover in vacant market stalls. I pass by a row of wooden stands that once housed souvenirs and games but now lie rotting.

My feet stir up dust with every step. I squat and touch the earth, grabbing a handful of the soil. Dry, lifeless. It flows through my fingers. Where am I?

I wander through rows of crumbling games. A small purple tent has a sign: "Bearded Lady 1 nickel. You won't believe your e..." The paint peels off in splintered chips.

Rounding a corner, I spot the big top. The massive red and white canvas is faded and torn. Light seeps from gaping holes. I edge closer.

Vance laughs quietly to my right. I turn and find him sitting on a bench in an ancient carousel. The macabre horses lack heads—as if a madman had come along and chopped them all off in a cruel practical joke.

My heart races, and adrenaline courses through me as I prepare to run.

"Wait," he says. "You always run. Why not stop and chat like civilized people for once?"

Is he trying to trick me?

I sprint toward the big top. A dilapidated flap door flutters, beckoning. Pushing the heavy canvas aside, I slip into the tent.

Inside, the lights flicker out. Stars surround me, breaking up the blackness. I creep toward a large table that's illuminated in the center of the room. I'm floating. Like I'm walking on air, but that's impossible.

I reach the table and inhale sharply. On it rests a model of Spark City. I recognize the tall skyscrapers, the enormous lake, and the river cutting through the center like a zipper.

Reaching out, I try to grasp the miniature living city, but my hands slice through the air. An illusion? Did Vance create this to amuse himself at my expense?

I step a few feet to my right, and the table expands, the city landscape endless. I bend, searching underneath, but find only black space.

Before I can rationalize things, a sharp tingling begins on my side. My fingers trace my old wound. A Heavy—the aliens that invaded Earth—stabbed me there years ago when I was in the war.

I glimpse down at my side, lifting my black t-shirt.

My skin around the wound glows blue. Pressing inward, underneath my skin, the alien blade remains.

Pushing my shirt down, I gaze up as a dark shadow falls across the Spark City replica. In the middle of the city, the earth is scorched, flattened. Glass towers, streets teeming with markets, bright neon lights. Gone. Reduced to rubble.

I back away, confused, until I bump into a tent wall. Fumbling for the flaps, I stumble out into the night.

Vance must still be around. I drop to a runner's stance, ready to bolt, when the old carousel organ starts up. Vance snaps his fingers, and the lights on the ride switch on. The carousel groans to life. Rusty wheels grate noisily as the contraption revolves.

"Come aboard," he says. "You can jump off and run whenever you want."

Now's my chance to escape and get a head start, but I'm so tired. The running is endless. Can I end the chase if I face him?

The carousel picks up speed. Suddenly, the carnival bursts to life around me. Light shines all around; everything looks pristine, no longer abandoned and rotting.

Strangest of all, people mill around dressed in clothes from a long-ago era. Men wear black suits and bowler caps; women wear long dresses and bonnets. Children run through the grounds, laughing and shouting in delight.

The carousel spins, and Vance remains dressed in his usual black pants and long, gray trench coat. I gaze down to be sure I'm still wearing my modern clothes too, including my familiar black combat boots. Nobody seems to notice us until I feel a tug on my jacket sleeve and find a little boy at my side. He's maybe eight-years-old and wearing a cap, white button-down shirt, and red suspenders that support baggy trousers.

"Excuse me, ma'am," the boy says. "The man on the carousel told me to give you this." He offers his hand.

Vance is malicious. Whatever it is could hurt the child. I shove his hand down. "No. Dangerous."

He peers up at me, eyes and mouth wide.

I bend down to inspect what he's dropped. A yellow rose lies at his feet.

The boy slowly edges away, then pivots and runs. I should flee too. But what if I stay and stand up to Vance? Will this endless chase stop?

It's worth a try. What do I have to lose? *My life.* A chill races from my fingers to my neck.

Treading cautiously to the carousel, I pick a spot five horses away from Vance's bench and leap onto the revolving platform.

"Well, I can't hear you from that far," he says. "Won't you come closer?"

"What do you want from me?"

He studies me with his half-metal cyborg face. He concentrates as though he can will me to come closer.

The hairs on my neck rise, and I shiver despite the mild air. There's something about Vance I can't remember. "How did we get here?"

"Here." He smiles. "We've always been here. And we'll always be here."

The carousel spins faster now. I shout to be heard over the din of the organ and the sound of people talking, laughing, living. "I don't understand."

"You will in time."

"How do I make this stop?"

He straightens against the ornate carousel bench, right leg crossed over his left knee. The carousel revolves so fast now that the people outside blur. We're the only passengers.

"You can get off the ride anytime you'd like." He shrugs.

Is this a puzzle? Clearly, he's more in control of this situation than me. I've been the one running, after all.

I stare down at the carousel floor to steady myself. I can't see the ground outside anymore because the ride spins so fast. If I jump, I could get hurt. Most likely, I'll fall off and land on something that would impale me. Hurting me—that's what Vance wants.

I'm so busy concentrating on the ground outside, trying to find a safe spot where I can jump, I don't realize he's moved until he grabs my arm with his cybernetic fist. My muscles tense, rigid as an icicle.

After months of running, he has me.

"Ida," he says between clenched teeth.

Perched on the carousel's edge, I angle my head to face his cold blue eyes and crimson pupils. His eyes hold a clue to my past. I can almost put my finger on it—retrieve the memory—but then it disappears into nothing.

"You don't remember the time before this place, do you?" His steel digs into my flesh, tearing the leather of my jacket. "Perhaps you will recall one day, but know this…" He gets so close, he's whispering in my ear. "I am part of you now…forever."

I'm disgusted by his breath against my cheek. It's ice cold, not what I expected.

His proximity, the speed of the carousel—I'm light-headed.

Vance pulls me closer and touches my right side, my old stab wound, with his other robotic hand. "The truth is inside you." He laughs, a deep, guttural chortling that unnerves me.

Outside the furiously spinning carousel, a bright flash crosses the sky. Lightning?

Vance presses his nose in my chin-length red hair, inhaling deeply.

"What did I see in the big top? What was the shadow on the Spark City replica?"

He whispers, "War is coming."

Shuddering, I glance up at another bright light, only this time, it doesn't dim. Like the aurora borealis, it floats in the atmosphere.

Outside the carousel, I hear voices. Loud, like people having a heated discussion. Two or three voices rise above the noise of the carnival and the out-of-control ride.

Vance's grip loosens, and he drops my arm. With a

devilish grin, he backs away, weaving through the decapitated plaster horses, and then he's gone.

I'm shaking and wondering how to get off the ride. Where did Vance go? Strange, he's never left me alone before.

I grip the pole of a horse on the edge of the madly spinning carousel. Outside, the bright light shines. Warm, welcoming.

I'm tired of running.

I leap from the carousel into the light.

Chapter 2
Masalai

"How does this work?" a young woman says. "We've been at it for hours."

A different woman, her vocal chords bearing the strain of many decades, replies, "Patience, young one." She speaks slowly, without wasting words. "The masalai poison is strong in her. Takes time to pull out."

I recognize the voices from the carousel before I jumped. Now they're close, as if I'm in the same room with them.

But that's impossible. Darkness lies before me, endless and all-consuming. And everything's gone— the carousel, the amusement park. Even Vance.

I'm still. Finally, no more running. There's just one problem. I can't move at all.

My body's numb, and my mind screams over the agony of being paralyzed. The worst part: being able to think and hear everything around me, but my eyes feeling like they're glued shut.

The old woman mentioned poison. Is that why I can't wake up?

Then I hear the unmistakable sound of a door opening, and a different woman says, "How are things going, Lucy?" She sounds kind and concerned.

Lucy. I recognize the name, but I can't place the memory. Somewhere a train whistles. It's miles away and sounds oddly comforting, even familiar.

"Alkina says we must be patient. She's working on drawing out the poison—the evil spirit—from Ida's body."

The one named Lucy says my name as if she knows me well. Why can't I remember her? These people are taking care of me. I must be very sick. How long have I been ill? I've been running from Vance for what feels like years.

"We have to feed Alkina and let her rest, Lucy," the friendly woman says.

"I know, Mom, but can we stay a little longer? I really hope this time we'll wake Ida."

"Lucy, please. Alkina has been working for hours without food or sleep. Come eat. You must be starving."

The old woman says, "Clever women don't eat when cleansing a body. We…what is the word?" She pauses. "We speed."

Her words hang in the air.

"You mean *fast*," says Lucy. "Alkina, the word is *fast*. When you don't eat."

Alkina mutters something in a language I don't recognize.

Cleansing a body? I don't understand. With all my effort, I will myself to move. Desperate, I want to scream, rise up, and push the old woman away. I rage inside against my useless limbs.

Nothing. Whatever energy I had while running from Vance has disappeared.

The kind woman's voice interrupts my thoughts. "Clever women. What does that mean?"

"Clever woman is her position with her people—the aboriginals. She's a tribe elder and a healer. Among her people, clever men and women cleanse those who have evil spirits." After a time, Lucy continues softly, "A healer for a healer. This has to work."

"Where on earth did you find *this* one?"

"Mom, you're not helping," Lucy says.

"At least let me bring you both some food?"

"No! Alkina and I are fine. Let her keep working on Ida. I'm not leaving until she wakes up."

Silence, followed by soft footsteps and the sound of a door closing. I'm left with Lucy and the elder aboriginal, Alkina.

I'm not familiar with the term 'clever woman.' A healer. Why has Lucy resorted to using her instead of modern medicine? Maybe I'm a lost cause. It wouldn't be the first time.

Next to what I assume is my bedside, Alkina chants, her voice soft, melodic, deep.

I drift off.

When I come to, blackness surrounds me.

And then it crushes me—the memory of Lucy.

My neighbor. A teenager, seventeen. We met and became friends. Well, sort of. She forced her way into my life and asked me to teach her how to defend herself.

The other voice was her mother, Vera, whom I saved when she overdosed on drugs.

And Gatz. My friend, I guess you could call him. A genetic mutant—half-human, half-wolf—he was unlike anyone I'd ever met. I remember him most of all, but I didn't hear his voice. Maybe he's not around.

A flood of memories rushes through me. As if transported, Vance appears in front of me. He's hardly human—nearly all his body has been transformed into a cyborg. We're in his factory where he manufactures his robotic army. He murdered Nancy —the woman I'd been searching for after he abducted her.

And he was going to kill me, too. No, scratch that. He was dying and wanted me to use my healing ability to cure him of his disease.

But he was a madman who had built a ruthless army of police androids. I had to stop him before he destroyed Spark City.

He would have hurt my friends. I had to protect them.

Lucy and Gatz came to rescue me. In the factory, they fought past Vance's androids and tried to help.

But I had to kill Vance.

Vance's voice erupts inside my head. *They're not*

your real friends. I am, he says. The sound chills me to my core. My pulse quickens.

I blink through wet eyes. The darkness doesn't seem so complete anymore. I detect the dim outline of a ceiling and a light above.

Lying in a bed, I try to wiggle my fingers for what feels like hours. One at a time, the feeling in my digits slowly returns. Progress.

Next, I try my feet. Yes! I can curl my toes.

What feels like an hour passes, and I lie in bed and twitch parts of my body one at a time. These tiny movements require all my concentration. My body drips with sweat by the end.

Finally, daylight peeks through the curtain of the window in my room.

I'm alive.

Chapter 3
Waking

Lucy finds me awake and conscious.

I loathe all the attention. She overreacts, starts crying, calls her mother, and sends video messages to Gatz. She's practically in hysterics, and I think she might pass out. I'm so hungry, and I don't have the strength for her frenetic energy.

"I have so much to tell you," she says. "I don't even know where to start."

Her mom intervenes. "Honey, give her time," Vera says. "She just woke up, remember?"

At my bedside, Lucy squeezes my hand too hard. "I'm just so happy you're okay." She adjusts the pillow behind me. "Are you comfortable? Can I get you anything?"

"Food," I say, my voice raspy from disuse.

Vera brightens at the mention of sustenance. "I'll get you something right away. What would you like?"

"Doesn't matter."

From the corner, the shaman woman interjects,

"Soup." Lucy and Vera both startle, as if they'd forgotten she was there. "Soup for her. Body weak," Alkina says.

"You know best." Vera stops on her way out and places a hand on Alkina's shoulder. "We owe you so much for waking Ida."

Lucy's still squeezing my hand and hovering close —too close. I can't take all this sudden scrutiny. I'm exhausted.

As Vera leaves the room, I spy a glass of water on the bedside table and turn my head, hoping Lucy gets the hint. She doesn't. Alkina notices and taps Lucy's shoulder.

"I can't even believe you're awake." Lucy holds the water glass to my mouth and lets me drink my fill.

I lie back on the pillow.

"You don't know how worried we were that you might never wake up. We tried everything— consulted with all the medical doctors we could find. Laser therapy, acupuncture, you name it." Lucy's long hair is tied in a ponytail, and she seems older, her face thinner than when I last saw her. "Gatz told me I was crazy, that you would wake up when you were ready."

Several minutes later, Vera enters the room with a small, steaming bowl. The unmistakable scent of chicken soup makes my stomach rumble. I don't care if it's dirty soap water—I want it. Lucy spoon-feeds me. Envisioning how ridiculous this looks, I vow to regain my strength soon.

Lucy continues chattering about the doctors, the renovations to my house, and her fight training as I eat. I try to follow but struggle. It's time to connect the dots. "How long?" I interrupt.

Lucy pauses with the spoon midway between the bowl and my mouth, then tips it to my lips. I swallow, letting the warmth flow down my throat. The broth is the best thing I've ever tasted.

Vera watches from the foot of the bed, but glances away at my question. What are they trying to hide?

"There'll be plenty of time for answering questions later," says Lucy. "Right now, we focus on getting your strength back." The spoon clatters inside the bowl. "Mom, we're going to need more soup. We have a hungry patient on our hands." She's unnaturally chirpy, her smile forced.

"Gatz?" I nod at Lucy's biocuff, which buzzes against her wrist.

"He's crazy excited that you're awake. As soon as he heard the news, he dropped everything, but he's far across the city…on business."

My heart sinks a little. It must be important business.

As if sensing my disappointment, she says, "Ida, a lot has happened since you've been asleep. We'll explain everything in time. It's a lot to take in all at once but—"

Her cuff continues its incessant buzzing. Lucy can't ignore it any longer. "It's him. Let me talk to him alone first and bring him up to speed. Then I'll bring in a tablet so he can holograph in. So he can see you." She springs to her feet. "I'll be right back. Okay?"

I manage a weak thumbs up. She leaves with Vera trailing behind her.

I'm left with the shaman woman, Alkina. She sits quietly in the corner, sizing me up.

"Tell me the truth." I figure she'll be honest while everyone else babies me. "How long was I comatose?"

"Year."

I let the word sink in. "A whole *year*?"

She pauses and assesses me with steely, weather-hardened eyes, shaking her head. "Two."

My God. What's happened in that time?

Chapter 4
Stubborn

Two years in a coma. Time wasted, never to be recaptured. I'm reeling, imagining all I could've done. Maybe I could have relocated and finally started my new life—the life I'd dreamed of before Spark City.

I study Alkina. The shaman, or "clever woman," as she prefers to be called, has a round face and wrinkled skin. Her nose and eyebrows stand out, but what I'm drawn to most are her luminous brown eyes. "Where are you from?"

"Australia."

I nod. As she gazes at me, I get the feeling she sees deeper than most people.

"I waited for you. Long time." She folds her hands in her lap. "I wanted to give up, but the girl did not let me."

"That would be Lucy," I mutter. "And yeah, she's stubborn. There's no changing her mind."

"She cares for you." She tilts her head, jostling a tangle of curls.

"How did you get me to wake up?"

"Was hard. You stubborn too. Took a long time, and I'm old."

I can't help but wonder how long she's been attending to me, trying to heal me. Lucy had tried many things. Where did she find this woman?

"Have you helped many people like me?"

"Some."

"I felt like I was in a dream the entire time. Is that normal?"

"Sleep is different for people." She leans forward, slowly raising herself from a comfy green armchair in the corner. "You had dreams. But he was there too."

My mouth turns dry. "What did you say?"

"The Metal Man. I saw him when I tried to wake you."

"How's that possible? I was dreaming."

"Not a dream. He's real. Still inside you. I couldn't get him out."

Chapter 5

Changes

Just as I'm processing the fact that this strange healer woman has somehow seen Vance in my dreams, Lucy bursts into the room and thrusts a vidcomm tablet on my bed. A digital image of Gatz emerges and hovers a foot above the screen.

"I wake up from a coma and you can't be bothered to stop by?" I say. With the soup and the shock of the old woman's words settling in, I'm getting my feistiness back. Gatz can handle it.

"Ida," he says. "When Lucy told me, I couldn't believe how lucky we are." He sounds choked up. "I'm so glad you're awake."

It's been a long time since I've seen his wolfish face. Gatz was a victim of genetic engineering when he was young. The scientists, if you could call them that, created half-human, half-wolf hybrids in China many years ago. Gatz made it out, barely, before the laboratory was destroyed.

From a distance, he resembles your average six-foot-two, well-proportioned human male. But close up, you notice beastly differences. Dark, shoulder-length black hair frames his sharp jawline, hiding sharply edged ears. Thick, wide-set eyebrows reveal intense, golden eyes.

Grinning, he flashes a mouthful of sharp teeth, with gleaming large canines. He wears his beard longer now instead of his former stubbly look.

Spark City is a haven for genetic hybrids like Gatz. Before meeting him, I'd been suspicious, even fearful of them. Many humans were. I'd certainly never gotten to know one.

"Is your schedule so busy, you can't make an in-person visit?" I run fingers through my hair and wonder how I look. Earlier, after realizing my gloves were missing, I made Lucy find them. My hands felt naked without them. Old habits.

A dark look crosses his features. Is he hiding something?

"Kidding, Gatz. Long time, no see."

He chuckles. "I'll say. When you don't want to wake up, you're a tough one to rouse."

"I needed my beauty sleep."

"It worked," he says, and my stomach does a flip.

"The gang's together again," Lucy says with a huge grin, sliding next to me onto the bed and mugging for Gatz.

"Y'all have way too much energy for me. Remember, I've been lying on my ass for two years."

Out of the corner of my eye, I register that Alkina's gone. Now that I'm awake, I wonder if she'll be sticking around. How did she know about Vance? I've got to talk to her again.

But Lucy doesn't give up. "The Triple Threat Trio is together again!"

"What are you talking about?" Gatz asks.

"I'm talking about us. Duh. The three of us are going to wage some badassery in this city."

He clears his throat. "Lucy, do you mind giving me and Ida a bit of private time?"

Her smile fades. Deflated, she mumbles, "Sure," and stalks out. With a last glance at me, she closes the door.

Alone with Gatz, I want answers. "What's the deal? Everyone's babying me. I may be weak right now, but I can handle the truth. I know I was in a coma for two years. What's happened?"

"There's a lot to explain, but are you sure you want to hear this so soon? I mean, you just woke up. Maybe we should get a doctor."

"From what I gather, the doctors aren't worth crap. If you need something done right, the medicine woman is the one to call."

"Lucy was right about her. I had my doubts. This time, I'm glad I was wrong."

"So, fill me in on the last two years." I'm desperate for information. I feel like the only one not invited to the party. "But wait. First, I need to know. The night I fell into the coma—Vance. What happened to him?"

"Dead. His body had been burned from the inside out. Whatever your touch did to him, he's gone for good."

I'm relieved to learn of his demise, but I still wonder why he was in my head during my coma. "What happened after that?"

"I went in. Took a team of hybrids and scientists with me into his buildings, his factory. We studied Vance's androids and plans."

The robots were a menace to the city when Vance took over the human police force, replacing them entirely. Composed of the cybernetic steel he invented, the machines were humanoid and stood seven feet tall. I fought them in the planetarium. One of them lunged for me, nearly throttled me, its lifeless round head showing no emotion. Only a red pulsating light scanning me behind a steel-gray visor.

"We worked fast," Gatz continues. "I wasn't sure how much time we'd have before the government—the military, actually—would claim jurisdiction. Sure enough, a week later, they seized his droids and took control of DremCorp towers. I fought to stay, but they wouldn't allow me or the others in, claimed they needed to study his technology for the advancement of science and to fight the Heavies." He wrings his hands. "You know how much I trust scientists. The military's here in the city. You might find it hard to believe, but I'm the mayor. Well, I was..." He lowers his head. "And now, I'm not."

"How's that possible? How could you be mayor? You're a—" I stop, realizing my mistake.

"A hybrid? Thanks for the vote of confidence." He crosses his arms. "I did a damn fine job, by the way."

"Sorry." I choose my words more carefully. "It's a

lot to take in. So many people distrust hybrids. Or, well, they did."

"After Vance died, the remaining politicians and city leaders appointed an investigatory committee. Several of us put our names in to become acting mayor. I figured the worst that could happen was a rejection. After a lot of vetting and intense interviews, it came down to me. I got a lot of credibility for helping take Vance out."

"And for two years you've been mayor?"

"Yes. Only now I'm not, because the military's in charge."

"What?"

"Spark City is under martial law as of last week. I was told to step down or be forcibly removed."

"Why?"

He frowns. "Ida, I know this is a lot to take in all at once. If you're tired—"

"Don't baby me." I bite my bottom lip. "Whatever's going on, I can handle it."

The hologram of Gatz flickers. "Let me show you." In his apartment, he strides to a window. "Open shade," he commands. A metallic panel slides open, revealing a city view. I squint, momentarily blinded by bright daylight. After a few seconds, my eyes adjust. In the distance, marine airships drop off supplies next to what appears to be a military checkpoint just outside the entrance to Section H.

Lucy barges in, scans the holograph, and jumps into Gatz's view. "You told her already? You were supposed to wait for me!"

I shake my head. "What am I seeing?"

Gatz explains, "The military swept in, led by Colonel Will Hunter. He's behind removing me from office. He's said hateful things about hybrids."

"He's a serious creep," Lucy interjects. "And worst of all, he's Paul's uncle!"

I take a breath. Paul had been Lucy's neighbor—another teenager her age. But he'd been more than an acquaintance. I'd saved his life after he'd been shot by a crazed former marine in downtown Spark City. Then I resuscitated him again after Vance shot him in the chest to "test" my healing ability. "Why would he declare martial law? On what grounds?"

"News from across the world is the Heavies are showing signs of returning. Authorities suspect reinforcements may arrive at some point. Colonel Hunter claims martial law is a matter of security. He wants to fortify the city, prepare a defense, and manufacture more of Vance Drem's robots to serve as soldiers on the front lines."

"Okay. But why couldn't they have done that with your cooperation as mayor?"

"Because he's the worst." Lucy huffs and folds her arms.

"Like I said, Hunter's fearful of hybrids and he's stirring up public outrage against us. In fact, he's been holding rallies and press conferences, saying hybrids are the downfall of Spark City. The press is having a field day, airing interviews where he says we've stolen jobs from humans and shouldn't have the same rights." He winces. "That we matter less than humans."

"Yeah. The hybrids are protesting against Hunter, but now angry human idiots are looting hybrid businesses, gathering into mobs, and rioting to drive the hybrids out," says Lucy. Her face grows serious. "Tell her the other part."

"Another time," he says.

"Tell me now. I can handle it."

Gatz sighs. "I've received death threats."

My pulse rises. "Is it Hunter's doing?"

"There's no way to know for sure," he continues. "Could be angry folks that have been stirred up."

"And? Go on," Lucy says.

He looks embarrassed to recount the details. "I told Hunter about the death threats and asked him for help. Tried to see if he'd tone down his message."

Smart. The military commanders I knew from wartime would rise above the melee and try to bring peace to the situation. "And what happened?"

"He told me it was the will of the people. That I should seek shelter in Section H. Hunter said hybrids should keep to ourselves and stay away from humans. We had little choice. After a few ugly incidents where hybrids had to defend themselves, all hybrids were sequestered to Section H at Hunter's command."

I flinch. "All of this because of one man?"

"One very powerful man who's taken over the city," he says. "I would be by your side in an instant, but every way in and out of Section H is guarded."

"We're going to take Hunter down," says Lucy. "Badassery!"

I'm nauseous. So much has happened, and I was asleep through it all.

Don't forget you caused all of this. Vance's voice booms between my ears, loud as a bullhorn. How can this be happening? I grasp the blanket in my fists and groan. *You triggered the downfall of Spark City when you messed with me,* he says.

"Are you okay, Ida?" Gatz raises his thick eyebrows.

Vance shouts, *You should have healed me, not murdered me!*

I dig my nails into my palms, manage a weak smile. "Yes, just need to rest."

Lucy and Gatz nod to each other, and he signs off after agreeing to check in later. "Get some sleep," Lucy says as she pulls the blanket over my chest.

She leaves, and I burrow under the covers, but sleep doesn't come.

Vance won't stop. *Oh, Ida. Don't forget, I'm a part of you. Can't wait to find out what you destroy next.*

I pass out to the sound of his laughter.

Chapter 6
Assignment

A couple of days later, I'm wide awake and restless after the current events update. "Asleep for so long. Time wasted," I mutter under my breath.

Gingerly, I lean forward and sit upright on the bed, lifting my arms over my head for a long glorious stretch. I've been sedentary too long. Will I have the strength to walk? Only one way to find out.

Flipping the covers off my lower body, I twist and hoist my legs over the side of the bed. I pause and catch my breath, taking in my surroundings. Home, only different. The place I broke into, where I squatted when I arrived in Spark City, was a long-abandoned dome-shaped conservatory surging with overgrown vines. Bordering the deserted zoo, it was a trash pit and unfit to live in. I never intended to be here long, much less two whole years pulling a Rip Van Winkle.

It seems Lucy and Vera cleaned up and renovated

while I was out of it. I peer up at the glass window-panes, repaired and recently scrubbed. Green coiling strands of kudzu vine once suffocated the ceiling, blocking most of the sunlight. But they've been trimmed. What was once all open space littered with trash and debris now has actual rooms—partitions that allow for privacy and individual sleeping quarters. Beside my bed, a nightstand holds a small digital tablet and a few dog-eared paperbacks.

I inch forward, plop my bare feet on the art deco green ceramic tiles. Cold. Just like I remember. Testing my weight, I nudge my body forward while resting my upper body on my arms. Shaky, but I'll be okay.

I manage several steps before Lucy storms in. "Hey," she says, cheeks flushed. "Why are you out of bed? You could've fallen!"

"Forget it. I'm fine." I amble across the room. "See."

"Amazing," Vera says from the doorway. She carries a tray with a teapot and mug and sets it down on the small table. "To be up and walking already…I wasn't expecting you to recover so fast."

"It must be your nanotech, Ida," Lucy says.

"Nah." I sidle to the bed and climb back in. "I've always been quick to recover. Just lucky, I guess." I nod at the tea. "I guess this place has a kitchen now?"

"Yes, it was all redone," says Vera as she pours. "A *lot* was done. Wait until you see it all."

I attempt a smile. I should be grateful. They lived here as they took care of me. Why not make it a nicer place? But where did the funds come from? Now I owe someone. Probably Gatz. I hate owing people.

"What's on the agenda today?" I ask after a sip.

"Since I alerted him you're awake, Major Tyren has been pinging every few hours asking to visit you."

Tyren. My old commanding officer. One of the few people on Earth I trust with my life. One of the few who knows about my ability. "I'd love to see him."

"I knew you would, but I've been holding him off." She smirks.

I arch my eyebrows. "What's up?"

"I'll message him, but on one condition."

"Go on."

"You promise to give me fight lessons again. I've been training like mad!"

"Are you crazy? I just woke up from a coma and you want to fight me?"

"Not today." She rolls her eyes. "Soon as you feel up to it. I've been practicing—every day." Grabbing my hand, she squeezes. "I really missed you. Everyone said you were a lost cause, but I knew better."

Swallowing hard, I blush at her sudden affection. I never had sisters, never knew my mother. "I'll do my best but go easy on me."

Tyren arrives a few hours later. I can't believe my eyes as I greet him at the door. He wears his military uniform. I grin at the sight of a familiar friend, one who survived battles and near-death experiences with me, and hug him.

"As soon as I found out you were awake, I wanted to come visit," he says.

"It's great to see you." I can't stop smiling.

Tyren has changed little over the years. His huge hazel eyes stand out among the sharp features on his dark face. He's as fit as he was in the desert.

He gazes past me to Vera and Lucy, lingering behind us. "Where are my manners?" I introduce them as my friends, awkwardly. "Meet Major Reginald Tyren."

"Nice to meet you." Vera shakes his enormous hand.

"Hi," Lucy says softly.

"Nice to see you in person, Lucy," he says.

"Would you like to come in for tea?" asks Vera.

"That's very kind of you," he says. "But I'm here on business and need to talk to Ida. Can we take a walk?"

"Yeah, sure. Let me grab my jacket." As I amble into my bedroom to grab my leather jacket, I wonder if he'll tell me why the hybrids have been sequestered. And why the city's on the brink of war?

Careful. It's Vance's voice in my head. *What does he really want from you?* he asks.

I shake my head in disbelief. His voice makes me shudder. Is it a side effect from my coma? "I must be going crazy," I mutter as I close the bedroom door.

Tyren and I set off outside into a light drizzle. Above, sweeping gray clouds blanket the sky. We stride in silence, and the moisture on my skin feels refreshing as we cross the grass. A long expanse of what was formerly dirt and dead weeds is now a neat, lush garden, thanks to Lucy. Buds are emerging from bushes and trees.

"Impressive," says Tyren. "Your new digs are interesting." He glances at the pale green dome-shaped structure. Built in the 1890s during a time of restoration following a massive fire, it once housed thousands of exotic plants, trees, and flowers from around the world.

"My place isn't for everyone, but it suits me."

"You always did things your way."

I scrunch my eyes and chuckle. Then, I remember the city is under martial law, and my smile disappears. "So, what's going on? What's happening with the military presence here?"

He frowns. "Bet you didn't expect to wake up and be told I was here, along with ten thousand of your fellow troops. I certainly didn't expect to be having this conversation either."

I shove my hands in my pockets, silently agreeing about the strange turn of events.

"Heard you got yourself into quite a mess when you moved here."

"Yeah, no kidding," I say. "Why are you stationed here?"

"Colonel Will Hunter. You know of him?"

"The jerk who kicked the rightful mayor out of power, sequestered the hybrids, and is stirring up hatred? Yeah, I know of him. I'm friends with Gatz, by the way."

"So I've been told."

"Tyren, everything that happened before my coma…It's a long story. A complicated one."

"I was briefed on your story."

"Really? By who? If it was Hunter, your information was probably full of lies."

"Look, Ida. Put your grudge aside. We believe the hybrids stole technology from DremCorp. It looks like Gatz was involved, and that's why Hunter wanted to remove him from power. He's been building a case."

"What kind of tech?"

"Based on archived records we unearthed from Vance Drem, we believe it's some type of mech suit. An armored suit with AI that he was testing. Early stages."

I wouldn't put it past Vance. Even in my hazy state, I'd seen all kinds of tech inside his massive underground factory. "Why the hybrids? What proof do you have? Maybe someone else stole it."

"Gatz and others like him had a full run of the DremCorp towers before we arrived. We found many signs that Drem's computer matrix had been hacked and exploited."

I kick the wet ground with my boot. "Why are you telling me this?"

He furrows his brow. "Hunter wants you to rejoin the military."

Cat's out of the bag about your power, Vance says. I clench my teeth as we stride through the wet grass, trying to block his intrusive commentary. *I'll bet Hunter wants you to serve by his side,* he says. *Heal him if anything bad should happen.*

"Have you thought about next steps?" Tyren says. "Now that we're here in Spark City, it seems logical that you'd serve with us. Hunter and I know what you're capable of. Your talents."

See what I mean? Vance says. How about the medical lab where you came from? Ask him what happened to that?

"I haven't had time to think yet." I shake my head, trying to quiet the intrusive voice. "Now that I know you're here…Yeah, I guess I could rejoin. It's just been a long time, and I haven't been myself."

He halts and faces me. "I missed you, Ida. I never realized how much until you left. Isn't that always the way? You take someone for granted until they're gone." Grabbing my hand, he stares down, locking his gaze on mine. "You're like a daughter to me. Please come back."

I swallow, fighting a growing tightness in my chest. I never expected to see Tyren in Spark City or to return to military life, and yet it's the one place where I feel like I belonged.

The lab, Vance says. Ask about the lab.

I yank my hands away from Tyren and stagger back, surprised at the force of Vance's words.

"Are you okay, Ida?"

"Fine. Still recovering," I say weakly.

"I understand. This is all happening quickly."

"Tyren, the military lab in the desert. Where you found me all those years ago. What happened to it? Does it still exist?"

His eyes betray a flicker of recognition and something else—surprise? "The lab I pulled you from? It was shut down and destroyed."

"That's a relief." My shoulders relax, and I silently curse Vance for digging up bad memories.

He's a liar, Vance says.

Tyren crosses the expanse of weeds and wild-flowers that border my unique home.

Catching up to him, I breathe in the humidity and the pungent smell of the soil beneath my feet. "The more I think about it, the more I'm loving the idea. It'll be like old times working together, you and me."

He halts. "Here's the thing…"

There's always a catch, Vance says.

"Hunter wants you assigned under his command."

"What?" I ball my fists. "You denied it, right?"

He glances away, his lips pressed together in a tight line.

"No way. I can't possibly report to that man!"

"Ida, he's my superior. I made a case that you'd be most comfortable reporting to me, but he disagreed. I'm sorry."

I stomp in frustration. "He's inciting riots. I saw him on the news—"

"He said something on TV you didn't like? He pisses off a lot of people. That doesn't make him a lousy commander."

"What he's doing—turning people against the hybrids—is wrong." Flushed despite the cool rain, I continue. "You've known hybrids, Tyren. They've served under you. Tell me what he's doing isn't wrong—"

"Hybrids have *died* on my watch." The tendons in his neck flex. "Don't lecture me about the morality of hybrid discrimination. Politics aside, if the hybrids stole Vance Drem's tech, that amounts to treason against the military. What they stole is a weapon. A powerful one. We need it back. It could protect us against the Heavies, if, and when, they invade again. It's what's best for the city, for the lives of everyone here, including the hybrids. We want you to help us."

I lower my head. Could Gatz really be behind the theft of a weapon? My stomach lurches at the thought of working for Hunter. What if Vance's voice in my head doesn't go away? There's no telling what I might do or say with him shouting at me.

Tyren checks his biocuff.

But I'm not done with my questions. "My healing nanotech. Hunter knows?"

"Paul told him. Hunter is his uncle."

Figures. Since I'd saved his life twice, nobody could attest to my ability more than Paul.

I follow Tyren as he starts toward his air cruiser. The reality of the situation sinks in. Once again, a powerful man wants to use me. For his own protection? Is that why Hunter wants me to report to him directly? "What did you tell him?"

"I told him how good of a soldier you were. How you were not only a medic healer but also a strategist and wicked smart."

We reach his cruiser, a two-seater he can maneuver

through the air at fast speeds above the dense city street traffic. Rain sends water trickling down my face. My mind wrestles with the fact that I'll be Hunter's soldier, not Tyren's.

Out of nowhere, rage engulfs me. Crazed, out of control, I punch through the window of his flyer, shattering the glass and sending shards on the seats inside.

Raising my chin to the sky, I scream and clench my fists. My entire body is tense. Full of hate, Vance controls me.

Tyren grabs me by the shoulder and shoves me away from his cruiser. "Ida, what the hell is wrong with you?"

Vance feeds off my distress and manipulates my fear into impulses I can't control. I force myself to kneel and shove my hands under my knees as the fury subsides. "Sorry. I don't know what came over me."

He leans down cautiously. "What happened just now, soldier?"

"I've been stressed."

"Are you fit to report to Hunter? I know you've been a hellion in the past, but he will mess you up if you act like this. Do you need more time?"

"Just go, please." I eye the dome, hoping Lucy and Vera didn't witness my outburst.

Tyren brushes the glass from his seat and climbs into the cruiser. "Take another week to recover, then report to HQ. Get your rest. You'll need it." Before lifting off, he says, "I believe in you, Ida. Don't let me down."

I'm still on the ground, crouched on wet gravel. Even though the rain cools my skin, I'm sweating and scared of what Vance might make me do next.

He rises within me to speak.

I close my eyes and try to push him down.

But he laughs and says, *Push me away, and I'll come back at you harder.*

Chapter 7
Lesson

Two days later, the last thing I want to do is spar with Lucy, but she won't leave me alone.

"You promised."

"Yeah, I know."

"You don't want to be out of shape much longer, right? You didn't say much about your visit from Tyren the other day." She stares at me as we hike toward North Pond.

I stiffen. I've been trying to avoid her and Vera finding out I'm rejoining the military. That I'll be reporting to Colonel Hunter, of all people.

"You're leaving us, aren't you?" She pulls my arm, halting us, and forcing me to face her. "He was here because you have to go back to the military?"

I nod.

"When?"

"A few days from now."

She peers down at her purple tennis shoes. "They

don't waste time. Is this what you want? To return to the military?"

I turn and walk. "You ask a lot of questions, you know."

She hustles to catch up. "Well, is it what you *really* want?"

"It's complicated, all right? Gatz might be in real trouble, and I can straighten things out for him."

"In trouble, like how?"

"No more questions."

"But—"

"Or we don't fight. I mean it."

She shuts her mouth and quickens her pace.

After a minute, we reach the murky, wide pond. I breathe in the crisp, spring air as I stretch my arms high above my head, locking my fingers together. Lowering my arms, I spin around slowly, gazing up at the sun poking out between fleeting rain clouds.

Lucy warms up on a grassy patch while I stretch my hamstrings. Fighting practice gives me something to concentrate on. A chance to test my physical strength.

Lucy didn't stop her training while I was in my coma. Paul took over her coaching until he allied himself with his uncle; they stopped being friends once that happened, she told me with a pained expression. Had the two of them been a couple? After the falling out, Gatz hired a martial arts instructor for her.

Lucy hops up and jogs in place, a shine in her eyes.

"Take it easy on me," I say. "I haven't worked out in ages."

"I'll be careful, don't worry." She grabs her backpack and pulls out two smooth, golden-colored sticks. "Bamboo from China. Gatz gave them to me, and I've been training with them."

"Fighting sticks? I guess the student has grown up and left her teacher behind."

"I doubt it," she says, her arms up in defense as she bounces in place. "I'm not as good as you might think, but I'll get there one day. Take a stick. We'll each use one."

We bow, then circle one another. Our shadows glide in and around our feet as if waiting for their chance to enter the fight.

I weave to my right in a defensive posture. My eyes shift quickly to a flock of birds in the shape of a V, flying north now that it's spring. I'm struck by the gravity of all that's happened—Vance's death, the coma, and how incredibly lucky I am to be alive.

"Your hair is longer," she says. "It looks good." She swings her head, and her long braid flies up and over her shoulder.

"Shorter is better for serious fighting. Let's go." I'm impatient to start. Enough talk about hair.

We step closer, narrowing our small orbit. I grip my bamboo stick in my gloved right hand, my left arm raised, poised for defense. I pause, legs wide and coiled like springs.

Lucy mirrors my movements. Her fighting stance

has improved. The instructor did a good job of helping rid her of bad habits. Now she's more flexible, less rigid than when I first started teaching her.

I edge closer, then lunge forward, attacking Lucy with the stick.

She blocks me with hers, matching each of my strikes, fending off my blows.

I withdraw. We resume our dance.

"You've improved."

My compliment catches her off-guard, and she smiles. I take advantage of the moment to launch another attack. I lunge quickly and whack her on the shoulder.

"Ow." She jumps back, grabbing her shoulder.

I retreat. "Never let your guard down. Especially when your opponent flatters you."

"I guess you haven't lost your trickiness."

I toss my stick from one hand to the other. "Never underestimate your opponent. Someone at their weakest may be the most dangerous."

She cocks her head. "Is that so?"

"We'll see, won't we?"

She launches an attack. I deflect her blows with my stick. My footwork surpasses hers, even though I'm rusty. I remember advanced steps that make me quicker.

Then I fend off another onslaught, but as I draw back this time, a wave of dizziness hits me.

You're off balance. Vance's voice pierces my thoughts as if there's a megaphone between my ears.

I can't help it. I close my eyes and raise a hand to my head. Lucy attacks. Her stick connects with my thigh, and the blow stings.

She hesitates. "Are you okay?"

I try to calm my breath. "Yeah, good shot on me. I just…I have a migraine. They come on quickly."

"We can stop."

"No, let's keep going." I need my strength back. It's important, but strength won't help me if I can't control Vance's outbursts. "Your footwork is much better but try to lead with your left."

She shifts her stance. Having grown taller in two years, her figure is more elegant. Nimble and fast on her feet, she's more imposing as an adversary.

And now you'll run from your friends back to your beloved military, Vance says. *How easily Tyren manipulates you.*

Damn him. Why can't I get Vance out of my head?

Lucy seizes on my distraction. A blow lands on my shoulder. I recoil, try a counterattack. She blocks, then advances again. This time, I push her off.

"You're good with the stick. Your trainer must have been a good fighter."

"He was okay, but I didn't like him."

"Why not?"

"He had me do stupid stuff like clean his weapons and polish his shoes."

I stifle a laugh. "Why did he make you do that stuff?"

"I don't know. Gatz said I talked back."

"So he made you do chores because of your attitude?"

Lucy shrugs. "I guess. Anyway, he's gone now. I don't need him anymore. Now I have you. The teacher I should have had all along. My best—"

I lunge at her and land three fierce blows. I can't stop. My arms move on their own; I would never attack her so viciously, with such force.

Her eyes grow wide as she falls to her knees, shielding her head. It takes every inch of strength to stop. I loom over her, stick raised.

Finish her. I flinch at the sudden jolt of Vance's words. *End her now. You'll kill her eventually, anyway.*

Confused and dizzy, I stagger back. Lucy blindly jabs with her stick, smashing me in the face. Hard. My ears ring, and I tilt awkwardly to the left. Warmth covers my chin. My knees buckle, and I fall.

"Ida, I'm sorry!" Lucy drops her stick with a clatter and kneels in front of me. "I didn't mean to… You were coming after me really hard and—"

"Enough." Feeling my nose with caution, I check for any ridges, bumps. "You didn't break it."

"I'm really sorry. Nothing like this has ever happened before."

I pinch the bridge of my nose to stem the flow of blood. "Lucy, this is part of fighting. It'll happen to you someday." Still dizzy, I force my head between my knees.

Drops of blood splatter onto the dirt. Vance has left his mark. He laughs again but sounds farther away.

He hides somewhere deep in my mind and emerges when I least expect it.

I need to get rid of him, or he's going to cost me a lot more than a bloody nose.

Chapter 8
Dream Walker

Since the incident at the pond, my stomach feels like it's full of rocks. My chest aches with guilt. I attacked Lucy with violent force, but it wasn't me. Vance forced me to act. I can't think of any other explanation.

If he can interfere with my thoughts and control my actions, he's dangerous. I don't want anyone getting hurt, especially not Lucy, Vera, or Gatz.

I need help. A way to get him out of my head. Lucy told me where the medicine woman, Alkina, lives. They set her up in Vera and Lucy's old apartment a mile away.

I jog to the building and climb the eight flights of stairs as I did once before to heal Vera when she overdosed. The smell of bleach clings to the walls within the stairwell. Harsh fluorescent lights guide me as I ascend.

As I reach the door, memories of the night two years ago flood me. Vera on the couch, unconscious.

She was too far gone, but Lucy begged me to try. I brought Vera back from death.

Knocking softly, I don't hear a response, so I rap louder. Nothing. I test the doorknob, wondering if something's wrong. It opens, and I venture inside.

The smell of incense invades my nostrils. A dozen small candles light the room. The furniture is basic—a couch, a small dining table with three chairs, and nothing else. No signs of modern technology, no media screen. I doubt Alkina has a biocuff or a matrix-connected device. She probably led a simpler existence in Australia.

My eyes adjust to the dim light. Alkina rests cross-legged on the living room floor with candles forming a circle around her. Before her, ancient-looking stones lie interspersed at odd intervals.

With closed eyes, she seems half asleep though she sits straight. Is she meditating? In a trance? I stuff my hands in my pockets, wondering how long it will take her to notice me.

The room is comfortably warm, and a breeze flows through an open window causing the candles to dance, casting shadows on the walls.

"Sit." Her voice breaks the quiet atmosphere, and I jump. Lately, I'm on edge all the time, worried when Vance will next penetrate my thoughts.

Eyes still shut, Alkina waves her hand in front of her, an invitation.

"I didn't mean to interrupt—"

"Quiet," she says sharply.

I step into her circle and sit facing the small, round woman.

Her features are blank, peaceful. A white paste covers her forehead, nose, and chin. Three small white dots run across her cheeks, and a mass of curly hair frames the top of her head.

The stone in front of me is the size of my palm. I've never seen a rock with its dark magenta color.

"You came," Alkina says in a low voice, her eyes now open and trained on me.

"Lucy told me I could find you here."

"Your face hit?"

"Just bruising from sparring with Lucy earlier. It's nothing."

She smirks. "The girl did that? She's tougher than I thought." Her eyes brighten. "What do you need?" She points to herself. "Help?"

I nod.

"What is the problem? Is it the man I saw? The Metal Man?"

"Yes. He's in my head. I hear his voice, and I think I'm going crazy."

"I see." She frowns.

"Is there anything you can do to help me stop him?"

"When I tried to wake you, I saw the man that you speak of. I pulled you toward me." She closes her eyes and grasps a small blue stone in front of her. "You were spinning in a circle, yes?"

Spinning? She must mean the carousel I leaped from. "Yes."

"His name is Vance. I see him in my mind's eye. I almost pulled him away from you." Her eyes fly open. "He's a bad man, very dangerous. Masalai."

"What does that mean?"

"A dark spirit." Alkina stretches out her hands, palms facing up. "My medicine pulls out the dark one." She clenches her fists. "But in you, he stayed. I pulled you out, but I could not pull him. He lives inside you."

"What do you mean, lives inside me?"

I am part of you now, Vance says.

"This metal man, he is dead, yes?"

"He died two years ago when I fell into my coma." I gaze down at my lap.

"You killed him?"

"Yes," I whisper.

"That explains it. His spirit went into you at death. He stopped you from waking."

"He hates me. He's dangerous. Please, can you pull him out of me? Make his voice stop?"

She clasps her hands, rubbing them together slowly. "Hmm. Very difficult…"

"Why?"

"Let me tell you a story." She waves fingers through one of the candle flames. "There was a boy named Iritu who lived in my village. One day, after traveling through the deep forest, he became very sick. He had gone to a forbidden place—a cave in the forest. A masalai spirit flew into him like a dark shadow." Suddenly, the candle in front of her flickers out. "He was possessed by a dream walker."

"A dream walker?" I fold my arms across my chest, on edge.

"Masalai made the boy sleep like you, and the dream walker haunted the boy as he slept."

The skin on my neck prickles. "Vance chased me through my dreams."

"Yes, he is a dream walker now."

"So how do I stop him? Can you pull him out? Destroy him?"

Her brow furrows. "My husband, he performed a ritual on the boy." She stares at the magenta rock. "He drove the spirit out of Iritu, but the masalai took something from the boy."

I lean forward.

A tear falls, streaking through her white face paint. "The boy, Iritu, he was never the same again. Numb. Didn't play or love his family anymore. He journeyed into the forest one day and never came back. I fear the same thing will happen to you if I try such a ritual."

"I could become numb and emotionless like Iritu did?"

"And you won't heal anymore. I see the healing energy in you—the machines in your blood. The ritual will destroy them."

"What should I do?"

She pulls an old-fashioned matchbox from her pocket and lights the candle again. "I must think. Meditate." She pauses for so long, staring into the candle, that I wonder if she's gone to another place. "Running out of time, Ida." She places her warm, frail hands on mine and peers into my eyes.

In a few seconds, my eyelids grow heavy and close. Then I'm jogging through a Spark City street, away from the river, away from DremCorp. In the distance, Section H appears. Gatz is there with Lucy, Vera, and Paul. I sprint, knowing I must reach them.

Warn them.

An air cruiser descends from the clouds and jettisons a bomb. The district erupts. A blast of white heat hurls me in the air and tosses me onto my back.

Ashes fall all around me. I rise and shake my head. Blood drips into my eyes. Section H is annihilated. Scorched. Like I saw in the big tent.

I scramble up and race down the street, dodging debris. Bodies lay scattered on the road, Gatz and Lucy among them, their arms outstretched, mouths twisted. Their vacant, lifeless eyes stare at me.

My eyes open. Tense and sweating, I'm reeling from the vision Alkina conferred.

"Running out of time, you see," she says.

"Is that the future?"

Her eyes narrow. "It's one future. I will pull out masalai tonight—come here at midnight."

A chill runs from my arms to my shoulders and down my spine.

"Must be tonight," she says. "I can't help you after that."

Chapter 9

Choices

As I walk home, the waning sun warms my body. I can't face Lucy and Vera yet. Instead, I follow a familiar path into the forest, inhaling the wooded breeze. Leaves and pine needles crunch under my feet. The air feels fresh today. A quiet stillness you only find among trees. The foliage blocks out the rest of the world.

I need silence.

Winding my way along the path, I spy a little overgrown trail that looks recently trampled. On a whim, I take it about fifty feet down to the edge of North Pond. A small boulder serves as a good bench.

I take a few deep breaths, letting the air flow into my lungs. "Breathing helps calm you," Tyren used to say. Returning to military life appealed to me more and more. Routine. Predictable. Little time for over-thinking, and no risk of hurting my friends.

You get rid of me, and you'll lose everything, Vance

says. *You're coldhearted now, just think what you'll be without emotion. No friends. No joy.*

I bend over and hang my head between my knees, hoping the rush of blood will silence him. "If you won't leave, I have no other choice." I straighten. "Do you hear me, Vance?" I pace in a small clearing next to the pond. "If I'm going down, at least I'll take you with me."

I wait for his reaction. "Come on, Vance? What do you have to say about that?"

Silence answers me. "What the hell do you want from me, anyway?"

It's not what I want, he says. *I'm stuck just as much as you are. Like it or not, when you killed me, I entered your mind. I'm a part of you now.*

"Stop it. Shut up. I'm sick of you in my head."

The feeling is mutual, trust me, he says.

I dig my fingers into my scalp, wishing I could eradicate him.

Can I scare him somehow? "Vance, I'm getting rid of you tonight."

Good luck. Just remember what you'll sacrifice…your precious Gatz and Lucy. And another thing, don't you have questions about your healing tech? I can help you discover how they made you, he says.

"What are you talking about? Who's 'they'?"

You didn't ask your dear Tyren enough questions.

"You're just stalling, trying to save yourself."

Hmm. Suit yourself. You'll be rid of me, but lose those you hold dear. Honestly, I've no idea why you care so much about a mutant wolf and a teenage brat. It won't matter anyway, because they'll all be dead when Section H gets wiped out.

"That won't happen. Alkina said that was one future. Tell me what you know."

You can't possibly expect me to give up my secrets, do you? Vance laughs. *After all, you already murdered me once and you're threatening me again. Don't you see my conundrum?*

"I'm getting rid of you. You're destructive."

I'll leave you for now, but some parting advice. Colonel Will Hunter and your beloved Tyren. Careful those two. Have they told you the truth about their plans for you? Tsk. Tsk. You didn't ask enough questions.

His devious laughter fades, and I'm left in silence.

I'm facing a huge decision. On the one hand, Alkina can exorcise Vance, but I'll lose my healing power and become hollow—a shell of my former self. A massive price to pay, but I'd live without him. But I'll never find out what he knows about my healing nanotech. The truth will die with him.

At the water's edge, I kneel, peering down at my reflection, and then graze the water with my fingertips. The water ripples, distorting my face. Fish swim below. Hardy little creatures to survive frigid Spark City winters.

In New York, I hung out at a spot under a bridge when I was fourteen. To pass the time, I fed fish in the river, sparing crumbs from whatever food I'd scavenged from back alleys of restaurants or stolen from food pods.

Like Lucy, I worked odd jobs in warehouses and

factories, trying to scrape by. My family was a group of teen misfits, our home an old, abandoned post office. The place was crumbing around us, but we made it our safe haven. Two years passed, and I survived, more or less, until I was arrested for lifting meds from a pharmacy.

The system sent me first to a juvenile home/orphanage where I fought with anyone and everyone. Those in charge hated me so much, they made a deal with criminals to take me away.

Blindfolded on the journey, I wasn't sure where I was taken, and I ended up in a medical lab. On my only outdoor excursion, I learned we were in a desert with no sign of other human life. Nowhere to escape. No hope.

The pond reminds me of my long-ago bridge spot and my fish. Solitude. A time when I had control over my life.

Those years—my childhood on the streets, the lab, then the military—hardened me. But underneath it all, I crave peace and normalcy.

Lucy reminds me of my younger self—having to care for her junkie mother, fighting to scrape by. No wonder she wants me to teach her how to fight.

I wish I hadn't pushed her away so much when I first met her. But it's too late. So much has changed.

How can I get close to anyone now that Vance can commandeer my body? Lucy, Gatz, and Vera will be better off without me. I'll wander away like the boy in Alkina's story.

Then again, I can't shake the feeling that I'm better

off staying. Fighting by their side, even if it means I'm stuck with Vance forever.

Can I save them from the explosion I saw in my dreams?

As I follow the path home, I stop midway and tread over to the edge of the pond one more time, taking in the view. As I circle back, I run into Lucy coming from the opposite direction. Head down, her gait is deliberate, and she seems lost in thought.

"Hey."

"Hi." She sounds deflated, like something's zapped her usual peppiness. Not only that, her gaze darts about as if she's nervous.

"Where are you going?"

"Just taking a walk," she says. "Stuff on my mind."

"I'm heading back home. Want to join me?"

She nods, and we start off side by side in silence, keeping the pond to our right as we travel south. After a minute, curiosity gets the best of me. "What's eating at you?"

"Huh?"

"Something's wrong. What gives?"

She stops on the path, and I backtrack.

"I'm worried about you. When we sparred, and you attacked me. It wasn't like you to come after me that viciously."

I stare at her in silence, realizing I owe her an explanation.

"I've been searching my mind," she continues, "trying to think whether I said or did something to piss you off. To make you come after me like that."

She thinks I was *mad* at her. I could tell her the truth about Vance...No, still a lousy idea. "Lucy, I'm sorry I attacked you like that. It was my fault, not yours. Don't worry about it, okay?"

Her shoulders relax a bit, but she bites her lip. "Also, I saw you in the little clearing next to the pond."

"Just a few minutes ago?"

"Yeah. I started walking over to say hello, but I heard you talking, and I thought you were with someone. So I held back, but there wasn't anyone there. You were talking to yourself."

My stomach drops. I'm irritated she spied on me, but my bigger concern is that she witnessed me dealing with Vance.

She blushes. "Sorry, I should have called out. I didn't mean to intrude. But can you see why I might be worried?"

I prop my hands on my hips. "Yeah. You must think I'm crazy."

Her lips curl up in a half-smile.

How much can I reveal without making her worry even more? "Lucy, something happened when I was in the coma."

"What do you mean?" she asks, eyes narrowing.

I struggle for the right words. "Vance Drem was a

powerful man." Too bad I can't reveal just how forceful he really is. "The thing is, I've been having nightmares about him."

She looks at me with raised eyebrows.

"The nightmares happen sometimes when I'm awake."

Her jaw drops. "Really?"

It feels good to confide the truth, and I can't stop myself. "I see and hear Vance often, actually. What you heard by the pond was me talking to him. Telling him to go screw himself."

"Wow. What are you going to do? How will you get the dreams to stop?"

"I visited Alkina, and she thinks she can help me. But there's a catch." I pause. "My ability to heal—that may disappear—and I might have to leave Spark City for good." I omit the fact that I might be a shadow of who I once was—not the Ida she remembers.

"No!" She grips my arm. "There has to be another way, right? You won't be the same without your nanotech. *I* won't be the same without you here."

"I know the situation sucks. But if I keep seeing Vance, I'm afraid I'll hurt someone."

"Like you almost hurt me?"

"Exactly." I sigh. "I'd give up my ability if it means not hurting people."

Chapter 10
Control

"Alkina? It's Ida." I push her apartment door open. "You should lock your doors, you know."

No response. Inside, my eyes adjust to the darkness. Curtains drawn, the only light comes from six small candles. She meditates in the same spot as before.

"I'm here for the ceremony," I say softly, scanning the apartment. Piles of dirty dishes clutter the sink. A box of unopened candles rests on the kitchen counter. I recognize a dish from my house. Vera must be bringing Alkina food.

She ignores me. Is she all there? I wonder if she's in her eighties or even her nineties.

"Ninety-six." Her voice startles me. "I have ninety-six years."

"How did you...? Never mind. You really should lock your door. It's not that safe around here. At least, it wasn't a couple of years ago."

"What have I to fear? I'm old. I have nothing."

"Right." She could probably put a curse on someone if they tried to steal from her.

Alkina wastes no time. She beckons to the floor in front of her, and I sit cross-legged.

She wears a dark yellow robe that covers her from neck to toe, her tribal makeup washed away. Her hands glide over the candles and stones in smooth, elegant gestures; she doesn't appear nervous about the ceremony.

As I settle on the floor, she studies my face with brown, unblinking eyes. Restless, I transfer my hands from my knees to my lap, not sure where to place them. "So, what now?" I check my biocuff: 2355 hours.

Still time to change your mind. Remember, my secrets die with me.

I wince, my back muscles tightening.

"Metal Man, he talks to you now?"

I rub my temples. "Yes."

"I see something." She leans back. "Trouble in your heart." She takes my gloved hands and inspects them.

"He's in my head, and I feel like I'm going crazy." A weight is lifted from my chest as I confide the truth. "I can't control him, and he made me hurt Lucy. I could have really injured her."

Alkina nods, and the flicker of a candle is reflected by her pupils.

"But…" My stomach feels like it's full of lead. "I can't do the ritual. Vance knows information about my past. I—I can't do it."

Lowering her gaze and releasing my hands, Alkina says, "I knew. When you came in. I saw it in your eyes." Her mouth forms a thin line. "No ritual. Masalai stays."

"He knows something important. I feel it in my gut. He could have answers that help me stop the bombing and save many people. For me to purge him…it's too much of a risk."

"You understand he stays in you?" She grabs my hands again, squeezing them. "I can't help after this." She waves at the window. "Full moon is almost over, and my time is coming." She lets go and pulls a blanket around her shoulders.

"Your time?"

"I die soon."

"But, how do you—"

She shakes her head. "My people always know. Do not fuss."

I lower my head. Tonight is my only chance. How can I go on with Vance living inside me? What kind of life is that? His presence is a constant reminder of his death at my hands, and I know he'll try to cause harm and chaos. It's his nature. But I can't risk losing his secrets—if he's telling the truth.

Alkina drifts off in thought. "Ah," she says, her eyes shining. "A gift for you." She touches my forehead. "You train this. As I do. Train your mind."

"What do you mean? Like when you go into your trance?"

"Yes, that. You train mind. You have control. Go into the dream state to face the dream walker."

I lean forward.

"I show you now. Close your eyes." A low hum emerges from her small body.

I squeeze my eyes shut, not understanding what's about to happen. She's gone into her meditative dream-state again. But how am I supposed to?

Then blackness surrounds me. I try to walk, but it's like I'm underwater. My legs and arms are heavy pieces of lead. Slowly, the darkness transforms into gray, then deep blue.

I blink rapidly until shapes form around me. Then I'm standing on concrete. Cool air rushes around me, bringing smells of the city—food stalls making fried noodles, the lake breeze, and factory fumes.

In the distance, the tops of tall spiraling towers appear. I'm on a rooftop. I recognize it as Vance's penthouse deck.

I feel a tug on my arm. Alkina lingers by my side in her long yellow dress. I think of the little boy at the carnival and the yellow rose he dropped. Was it Alkina back then sending me a sign?

I hear her answer in my mind. *Ida, when you want to enter the dream trance, think of the yellow flower.*

"Okay."

Try it now, she says.

I close my eyes and picture a flower. A few seconds pass. "Am I doing it right?"

Nothing.

This time, I concentrate on the yellow rose that the little boy dropped, rotating it in my mind, remembering the smooth petals. A white light flashes, and I'm transported to another place.

Before my eyes, an incredible landscape looms. Above me, an endless red-orange sky stretches. On the horizon, a mountain rises from the Earth. The light bouncing off the atmosphere bathes the rock formation in an unearthly glow.

"Home. Uluru," says Alkina. Somehow, we've been transported to the Australian desert. "I leave you now. Come here when you need me." She treks across the desert toward the giant red rock.

"But wait. How do I find Vance? How do I control him?"

"Go to him," she says over her shoulder. "The Metal Man."

"How?"

"Go to the rooftop. Get the answers you seek there. You must take control of him. You will learn how…in time." She plods slowly away before halting. "Something else you must know. Come." She motions for me to join her.

I jog over. "What is it, Alkina?"

"Metal Man will test you. Will try to trick you. He wants to control you more than anything."

"Control me, but how?"

"No time to explain." She gazes at the setting sun as it bathes Uluru in sheets of golden orange shadow. "If you give him control, you will be trapped inside. Trapped like he is now." Her dark eyes penetrate the eerie stillness of this ethereal dream world. "You would be trapped forever, understand?"

"Yes."

Then she journeys away and fades into the distance. I'm left by myself, shivering and uncertain.

The rooftop. How do I return there? Did she mean physically go or travel in my mind? Confused, I shut my eyes, willing myself to snap out of this dream state.

A white flash, and I'm on Vance's rooftop again. Police sirens and beeping car horns fill my ears.

"Miss me?" Vance says from behind me.

I spin and brace myself, afraid he'll hurt me.

He leans against a waist-high glass railing, inches from the roof's edge and a sixty-five-story drop.

"You made the right choice." He grins. "I knew you would."

I straighten, hands on my hips. Alkina's right. I need to take control of the situation. No more running. "We made a fair deal, Vance. I didn't purge you. Tell me what you know about my past."

He shrugs. "That's the funny thing. I know nothing for certain."

I fold my arms across my chest, raise my chin.

"Simple deduction, really." He paces in front of the rail. "You were part of a rogue medical experiment for what? They changed your body surgically, subjected you to experiments. It's a crime what they did to you." He halts, staring at me. "I know they tried to make you kill people. I saw it in your dreams."

My mind races. How could he know? I've told no one, not even Tyren, about my years in the medical lab. How they made me and others shoot a guard named Peterson. My legs tremble as his tirade continues.

"The scientists in charge used you for an end goal. You ended up with an extreme healing ability. A handy tool for a military arsenal."

"What are you getting at, Vance?"

"Patience!" He waves his hand, the human side of his face reddening. "Arsenal. I keep getting stuck on that word. What's the military in the business of doing? Killing and blowing things up."

"Are you stalling?" I clench my fists.

He rushes toward me, fast on his feet, and the tendons in his neck jut out. "The military creates weapons against threats. That's what they do."

I step back, unable to hold his gaze.

"You were stabbed with a Heavies' blade and lived. How? Has anyone else ever lived after such an attack? I've never heard of survivors."

"How should I know? The knife lodged in me. It wasn't deep enough to kill me, I guess."

"The alien metal exists in your body. It's changed you. The blade inside you has lain dormant." He resumes his pacing. "And now you've emerged from a long coma and get back on your feet in a few days. Suddenly, your Tyren has taken a keen interest in you again."

"So what? He and I are friends."

"Right." He spins, and his dark gray trench coat flairs behind him. "The military's favorite lab rat has shown remarkable powers again. Tell me, who was behind the experiments and surgeries you had to endure?"

"It was a rogue operation. Scientists committing crimes. Tyren rescued me from it. He gave me the opportunity to join the military."

"Is that so? Have you ever asked him for the details of what went down? For instance, how he knew about you? His relationship with those in charge?"

"I don't need to. That's history. What's your point, Vance?"

"Humor me. What if the military was behind your 'rogue lab' the whole time?"

I shake my head. "This is what I risked everything for? Conjecture from a known psychopath? Screw you."

He raises his chin and laughs. "Don't count me out yet, Ida."

I cringe and cover my ears at the sound of his piercing, maniacal cackling. Closing my eyes to shut him out, his voice disappears.

Wincing, I open my eyes inside Alkina's apartment. No daylight seeps in from the corners of the curtains yet. My cuff reads 0230.

She's gone. Only her yellow dress and blanket lie on the floor in a heap. I scramble up and search for her. I check the bedroom, then the bathroom.

Vanished. *My people always know,* she'd said.

I fold her clothes and lay them on the couch before

blowing out two flickering candles. From the door-way, I take one last glance at the small apartment.

"Rest in peace."

Chapter 11
Theories

Morning light streams through my windows as I wake to the sound of my vidcomm sounding an incoming message. Sitting up, I rub my temples and unleash a yawn. After last night, I couldn't sleep and might have squeezed in an hour.

My mind spins. I can't believe Alkina's dead, but I know she's in a peaceful place. I can find her if I need to.

At least, I think I can.

She taught me how to enter the dream state. To confront Vance. My encounter with him was frustrating because he lied and tricked me. He doesn't have any real intelligence about my past or how to prevent the destruction of Section H. Worst of all, now I'm stuck with him. Bound to him.

My discarded biocuff rests on the floor next to the boots and jeans I kicked off in the early morning darkness. I roll over, hang my legs over the side of the bed, and place my bare feet on the chilly tile floor, then recoil. Vintage buildings retain the night's cold deep in their bones.

Groggy and bleary-eyed, I lift the device. Tyren's face appears. I look like hell, but I don't care; he's seen me at my worst. Pulling on my jeans, I tap the screen, and a holographic display lights up revealing him behind a desk.

"About time you answered," he says, one eyebrow arched. "Guess your time as a civilian has made you soft. Think you can sleep in?"

I wipe the sleep remnants from my eyes. "Rough night, Major."

"Out partying already?" He smiles. "How you feeling today? Health-wise?"

"Better. I guess. Just tired." After sleeping for two years, you'd think I could skip a night. "Not entirely myself yet."

"You'll be at full strength soon, I'm positive. In fact, we want you to report to headquarters this morning for medical observation." He leans closer to the camera.

"Today? I thought I had a few more days. Who's *we*?"

Tyren tilts his head. "Colonel Hunter's becoming impatient."

I tuck my feet underneath me on the bed. "He can wait, for all I care. Doesn't he know I just woke up from a coma?"

"Ida." His voice softens. "I know you're not happy about what's going on with the hybrids. They're your friends, I get it. This must be incredibly disappointing. But Hunter and the rest of us are here for a reason. We're trying to keep the peace. *I'm* trying to keep peace with Hunter, and you're making me look bad."

I lower my head. How can I give into Hunter? The thought of him makes my blood boil after what he's done to Gatz and the hybrids. And yet, hurting Tyren is the last thing I want to do.

"So, I'm asking you as a friend first, and as your superior officer second. We need you. Your military family needs you. Come back. We never should have let you go in the first place."

He's right. Vance's words were all theories, conjecture. Lies.

Tyren and my troop were the only family I've ever known. Catching his gaze, I relax my shoulders. "I'll report later today, Major."

He nods, and I switch off the comms. I hug my knees to my chest. What have I done? How will Lucy react when she finds out I'm leaving today?

And Gatz. I feel like I'll never see him again. Maybe it's just as well, because I can't imagine telling him I'm returning to the military—that I'm choosing the side against him and the hybrids.

After all that he's done for me.

But the military is home. It's all I've known other than my childhood on the streets and my short time as a civilian in Spark City. Left on my own, I managed to attract all the wrong attention.

I can serve as a medic again and convince Hunter that the hybrids deserve better treatment.

Chapter 12
Yellow

I can't put my finger on it, but talking to Tyren felt different this time. I know him so well, and he's never pressured me before. He's following orders, obeying his superior—he has to.

Leaning against the bedroom wall, I lower myself to the ground and cross my legs. Time to see if I can put Alkina's training to use. I need answers.

Closing my eyes, I picture the yellow flower. Blackness consumes my vision, and the yellow rose revolves slowly, like the carousel in my dream state. My eyes capture the details of every petal, each a perfect creation of nature.

Then I'm on the roof—Vance's penthouse, as it was years ago. Wind sweeps across my body, my hair whips my eyes, and I shove strands behind both ears as I take in the view. A dull gray sky looms overhead, obscured by massive clouds.

He's here, somewhere. Scanning the perimeter of the rooftop deck, I spot a shadow. I start toward it, then glimpse Vance's figure behind a pillar. "Come out," I order.

Emerging from his hiding spot, he walks toward me. "Well, well. A lovely day for a visit. How is the land of the living in Spark City these days?" He grins as the metallic side of his face reflects the roiling clouds above.

I shake my head. "No. I ask the questions today."

He shrugs and pauses two feet away. "Have at it. Not like I have anything better to do."

"Tell me what you know."

He tilts his head, smirks. "Well, I have a fondness for eighteenth-century British literature—"

"About the military and the medical lab. Tell me what you know."

"Has Sleeping Beauty finally woken?"

"Out with it. What do you know?"

"I wondered when the little orphan girl might get curious about what happened to her." He rocks back on his heels.

I lock my gaze on his cold blue eyes. His red pupils shine eerily.

"Shouldn't we have a drink? I'm awfully thirsty."

"Answer me." I clench my fists, hating how he toys with me.

"Okay." He rolls his eyes. "I've met Colonel Hunter before. A likable fellow, although rough around the edges." He pauses. "Is this what you want to hear?"

"Go on."

"Several years ago, before you murdered me,

mind you, I was invited by the military to a classified meeting along with several prominent scientists and wealthy businessman across the continent."

"What kind of meeting?"

"Patience, my dear, I'll get to the point. But first, I'd like a little treat. Ever since you killed me, I can't get the stuff I want. My treats." He smiles. "I want wine, champagne. Some scotch would be nice, too. You have no idea how boring it is here."

I roll my eyes. "Vance, I don't know how to get you booze. I barely even know how to get here."

"Hmm." He taps the side of his head. "Wish for it."

"No, that's ridiculous. Finish your story."

"Fine. For this military meeting, I was flown to a secret location. They blindfolded me for part of the trip. I felt hot, dry air when we landed, so I believe it was a desert."

"How long did you fly?"

"They served stiff drinks. I got woozy. They must've sedated me and the other passengers. It could've been four hours or sixteen. We get to a secret location, and we're inside a building. Maybe it was underground, but I'm not sure. It felt secure, like a bunker." He pauses. "I'd kill for a mimosa."

I grit my teeth, wondering how much time is passing in the real world. "Come on, finish the story."

"They talked to each of us, alone. For hours on end, they asked me questions about my androids. How did they work? How did I design them? What could they do? And so on."

"And you told them?"

"They wanted my secrets as a matter of national security. If I lied, they'd find me guilty of treason and throw me in jail." He grins. "So, of course, I lied through my teeth. I didn't want the military getting their grubby hands on my intellectual property."

"Who were these people?"

"Colonel Hunter stands out in my memory the most. He was definitely in charge. Others in the room were scientists, I assumed. They took notes, asked the technical questions. Oh, and your friend was there. Major Tyren."

How long had Tyren known Hunter? Is Vance lying and trying to get me to doubt Tyren's honesty? I served by his side for years. He's a good man.

I pace, trying hard to slow my racing thoughts. "So far, you haven't told me anything earth-shattering. The military was trying to find out about your droids. That's no secret. They've been searching for ways to defeat the Heavies for years now—ever since the invasion in the Middle East. It makes sense they would meet with scientists and seek the help of a businessman who was building a small army of robot warriors. You don't run across that every day."

"Yes, well. Suit yourself. You wanted to know what I knew." He shoves his hands in his pockets, whistles a tune.

"What gives? What are you holding back?"

"First, a treat."

"Vance, I don't know how to get you booze. I told you."

"I think you do. We're in your mind, right? Think, and it becomes so."

I swallow hard, feeling silly. Staring down, I imagine a bottle of champagne. Am I going completely nuts? I curse myself for listening to him.

"Yes!" He claps. At his feet rests an ice bucket with a bottle of champagne inside. "You did it. Bravo."

How was this possible? Someday, I'll try to figure this out—with lots of therapy—but right now, I'm running out of time.

"You got your present," I say. "Now tell me what else you know."

Vance pops the cork and takes a long swig. "Ah, that feels right." He wipes his mouth with his jacket sleeve. "They revealed some experiments they were working on. Of course, I was sworn to secrecy under penalty of death."

"Why would they expose anything classified to you?"

"Damned if I know." He throws back the champagne bottle and drinks. "They showed me several soldiers in training. Young. Maybe sixteen, seventeen years old. Boys and girls. Most were hooked up to machines, unconscious."

A hollow feeling grips my insides. Could it be the same place I was held?

"They were creating little monster soldiers. They showed me one boy who could knock down a brick wall with his mind. Imagine that kind of power. It seems there were side effects, however. After the display, the young man rammed his forehead with a brick over and over."

I want to vomit at the thought of what those scientists did to the boy. To others.

To me.

"The truth is," he says, downing the rest of the bottle, "you came from a lab. And your beloved Tyren was part of it."

In a rage, I punch him in the chest. He staggers back, dropping the bottle, which shatters. Grabbing his coat, I haul him across the four feet separating us from the tower's edge. I lean over him, his body weight teetering over the edge.

Underneath me, he grimaces, his body tense. "Face it. You need me."

My trembling hands let go, and I clap to wake myself.

Back in my room. Alone and rattled.

Tyren's words echo in my head: "We never should have let you go in the first place."

Chapter 13
Confession

Lucy is grinning. She hops from side to side in her purple tennis shoes. "I have a surprise for you."

Gatz bursts into my room, out of breath.

I smile at his familiar wolfish face, unable to help myself. "I guess hybrids don't knock."

"Ida." He practically leaps across the room. "I'm so glad you're awake." He takes my gloved hand, and I notice his sleek brown hair has grown past his shoulders. He wears it swept into a ponytail at the nape of his neck.

"Long time, no see."

"I'll say." He leans in for a hug, wraps his arms around my middle, and squeezes tight, hoisting me off the floor.

Under my hands, the muscles of his back feel solid. His beard, surprisingly soft, tickles my neck. He holds me for a few seconds before letting me go. I look into his golden eyes, then force myself to turn away before he can see me blush.

"If you were trying to get your beauty sleep, it worked."

"Times sure have changed," I say, ignoring his compliment.

He shakes his head. "No kidding."

Lucy fidgets. "You two have catching up to do. I'm gonna check on Mom."

"Thanks, Lucy," I say as she leaves.

Gatz pulls up a chair, and I take a seat on the bed. "How did you get here? I thought hybrids were sequestered."

"Some of us have passes to travel in and out on business. Even so, it's dangerous. Several hybrids have been attacked, gotten caught up in riots."

"And you have a pass?"

He shakes his head and stares at me with his intense eyes. "I had to see you in person."

I flush, not knowing how to respond.

"After Hunter rose to power, things got so bad, all the hybrids either left the city or moved to Section H, abandoning their homes and businesses." He lowers his head. "I had to ditch the bar and the mayor's office, but I'm the one in charge of H these days."

"That's good, I guess...About being in charge, I mean."

"Now that Hunter set up a military checkpoint outside H, I'm just trying to keep the peace as best I can."

My stomach churns. "Hunter sounds like a genuine piece of garbage."

He rises and paces the floor. "My people are getting restless."

"I can imagine."

"We're over capacity. Food supplies are low. The military's being a pain in the ass, as you can imagine."

Your military, Ida. Look at what your family is doing to your hybrid friends.

"Are you okay, Ida?"

I dig my nails into my palm. "Yes, I just get tired easily. Did you take something from DremCorp… before the military came? Some weapon?"

He flinches. "How did you know?"

"Tyren visited. Sounds like it's important enough they want it back."

"He told you what it is?"

"He said it's a prototype Vance had been working on. A mech suit with AI."

"Yeah." Gatz scratches his head with one of his claws. "It's a helmet that we believe wraps around a person to create body armor. We knew it was powerful based on the schematics we found. Only trouble is we haven't discovered how to activate it."

And they won't. They're missing the igniter, Vance tells me.

I shake my head. "You won't because you're missing part of it."

"How can you possibly know that?"

I avert my eyes. "Never mind. Hunter's searching for the mech helmet. Is it worth fighting for?"

"I don't want him getting his hands on it."

I don't blame Gatz. The helmet could be a bargaining chip for the hybrids, or if they could figure out how to use it, a weapon. "I have to report to HQ today…If Hunter asks me about the helmet—"

"Tell him I have it. Don't lie and get yourself in trouble." Gatz sighs. "You and I have a knack for getting ourselves into complicated situations, don't we?"

"How long can you stay?"

"I can't," he says. "I need to get back to H soon."

"It's dangerous. I'll ride with you."

"What? No way. I'll be fast. I wear a baseball cap, a high collar, and I flatten my ears." He grins.

"You took a huge risk coming here."

He grabs my hands. "Ida, there's something I need you to know."

I redden and glance away.

"I never gave up on you. Neither did Lucy. She deserves all the credit for bringing you back. She loves you like a sister, you know that, right?"

I nod, and I can hear my heart thumping in my ears.

"I never stopped hoping you'd wake up. I thought a lot about the future, about how brief life is and…" He squeezes my hands, his claws digging into my palms. "Ida, I—"

Lucy bursts into the room, out of breath. "Military patrol outside. They're approaching the house."

Chapter 14
Riot

In the common room, Gatz tosses on his baseball cap and peeks outside from one of the dome's glass panes. "Someone must have tipped them off."

"Maybe they just want to talk to Ida," says Lucy.

Five soldiers, fully armed, approach the front of the dome, checking their weapons. "This isn't your usual friendly visit." My heart races. "They must have been watching the house, knowing it would be a matter of time before Gatz showed up here."

"I parked my vehicle half a mile away. Took the path through the woods," he says.

"We'll take my motorcycle. I'll get you out of here."

"I can fit your bike in my truck. It's a mortuary van we use to travel outside H."

Lucy glares at me. "What about me?"

"We need your help," I say. "You've got to stall them. Think you can do that?"

Her face lights up. "I've got charm for days."

"We'll message you when we're clear. Be on the lookout and let us know what happens."

Lucy shoves Gatz toward the back exit. "Go." The soldiers bang against the front door.

Gatz and I stride toward the rear door, but I pull his arm down. "Duck." Soldiers flank the outside. "Come on," I say, crawling toward my bedroom.

The pounding continues as I shut the bedroom door. We hear Lucy at the front door. "Who is it?" she says, drawing out each syllable.

I peer through a window past a small group of trees. Twenty feet away lies the shed with my bike. "Are you ready?" I ask.

"Let's do this."

I push the window pane outward when he grabs my shoulder and pulls me toward him. "I didn't finish what I started to say—"

I clamp my hand over his mouth. "We'll have plenty of time later, okay? First, I've got to get you out of here."

He nods and we climb out the window, crouching behind the fledgling trees. By now, the soldiers have entered the house, and I hope Lucy is being careful. I have no doubt she can stall them, but will she be safe? I'm counting on her.

We scramble down a small, sloping hill to the shed. Using my thumb, I press the biometric device that secures my motorcycle inside. The lock gives and we scurry inside.

Darkness surrounds us, and I feel the wall for the

light switch. We hear a swishing sound once the light flickers to life.

"Mice?" Gatz asks.

I shrug. "Hope they didn't eat my engine wires." I grab the canvas covering the bike, pulling it off. My baby still has a shine from its last polish. I run my fingers along smooth red chrome, then grab the handlebars, pop the kickstand and climb on the seat. "Hop on." I toss him a helmet.

He settles on the seat behind me and wraps his hefty arms around my stomach, causing me to tingle up and down my spine. Was he about to say what I think he was going to say? No. I push it out of my head. For once, Vance has been quiet.

My bike's a one kicker, a finely tuned machine that usually starts on the first try. But now that it's been sitting for nearly two years, I don't know what'll happen.

"Don't worry," he says. "I took care of your bike. Regular oil changes, and I had my buddy take a spin once in a while. But the last time was two months ago."

"You did? Nice job. You may have saved our asses." After slipping on my helmet, I kick-start the engine. The throttle jumps to life, the engine purring. I rev it once, twice. Good to go. I squeeze the clutch, shift into first, and gun the bike through the unlocked door.

We careen out of the shed and down a hilly incline, moving fast. Ahead, a grassy field separates us from the wooded forest. Out of the corner of my eye, I glimpse the soldiers' surprised reactions. They sprint to their air cruisers in pursuit.

They'll notify Hunter and Tyren. Not only will I be in trouble for helping Gatz, I disobeyed a direct order to report to base. But I don't care. Gatz won't be captured on my watch. I'll get him safe; it's the least I can do.

We crash through Lucy's garden, knocking over wire cages holding tomato plants and flinging up mounds of soil.

"What are they doing?" I yell.

"They're on our tail. Hurry."

A foot away from us, a bullet ricochets, sending a torrent of grass and dirt flying. Why would they shoot at us? Tyren will be furious when he finds out.

I pull hard on the gas, and we fly at breakneck speed toward the refuge of the forest. More bullets shred the grass behind us. Then we're inside, among tall trees, out of view.

I know these wooded paths well; they were once a sanctuary. A place I could escape. We ride through the forest undisturbed. The air cruisers can't navigate the dense brush and narrow paths. I slow down so we can hear each other over the hum of the motorcycle's engine.

"Where do you think they'll try to cut us off?" asks Gatz.

"At the main road. Where the forest ends."

"So what do we do?"

"Can you handle more all-terrain travel?"

He laughs in my ear as he squeezes me tighter. "With you, I can handle anything."

I hook left, and we exit the forest and veer into a barren field. Unkempt, straggly prairie grass tickles our shins as we rocket through the deserted fields.

Massive solar energy towers lace our path toward the city. Just as I gaze up, worried about air cover, I spy the first drone. Have they seen us? I can't be sure, so I swerve to the left down a small ravine and cut the engine.

We jump off, lay the bike down, and crouch underneath overhanging old-growth trees. The minutes tick by as several flying drones scan the area.

"Think they saw us?" Gatz whispers.

My words come out in waves of anxiety. "Hey, next time you want to visit, drop me a note first."

He smirks. "Will do."

Finally, the drones give up and fly north toward the waiting air cruisers. We rise, brushing dust and dirt from our bodies.

Back on the bike, we travel slowly down a dirt service road. Before long, we reach a densely populated street with rows of high-rise towers packed with residents. Fortunately, the helmet disguises Gatz's wolfish features, and we traverse the busy street undetected.

Pedestrians, electric cars, bicycles, and a few other motorbikes jostle along the street in all directions. Weaving another mile, we reach a river crossing and approach a drawbridge when traffic grinds to a halt.

"Something's happening up ahead," says Gatz.

I crane my neck for a view. A small crowd has amassed on the bridge. Horns blare and frustrated people exit their vehicles. In the distance, there's angry shouting. I inch the bike closer, squeezing past stopped cars and receiving dirty looks.

A dozen men and a few women run toward a crowd assembled in the middle of the bridge. A few of the men wear masks and raise their fists. We can't pass because the group's numbers grow as more curious bystanders arrive on the scene.

Gatz leans forward, to one side. The crowd forms a circle. Enraged shouts fill the air.

"What's going on?" I ask.

"Someone's in trouble." He climbs off the bike, eyes wide. "Stay here. I'll check it out."

Ignoring him, I jump off and engage the kickstand. After a few feet, he peers back and shakes his head.

Men in the mob jump up and crash down again as if they're kicking something on the ground. The crowd is like an angry mosh pit—bodies hurling against each other, shouting, fists raised.

I grab Gatz's arm to avoid a collision with a man rushing up from behind. We end up jostling another man who stares into Gatz's visor and recognizes him. "Out of my way, hybrid freak," he yells.

Ahead in the crowd, a man wearing a ski mask and brandishing a switchblade points at us and shouts, "A hybrid! Let's get him!" Other men turn in our direction and advance. Several carry billy clubs.

Gatz bends down, reaches under his pants leg, pulls out a pistol, and waves it in front of him. He's not aiming at them, just displaying it, when he shouts, "Get out of here!"

The men edge away, and others flee the scene. The masked, knife-wielding man swears at Gatz and runs off with his fellow attackers.

Once the crowd disperses, we see a body lying on the road surrounded by debris, including broken boards and glass. We race over and discover a badly beaten woman.

"That's a soldier's uniform," I say.

Gatz gently rolls her onto her back. She's bleeding profusely, blood pooling on the ground around her middle. Stab wound.

"How could anyone do this?" My voice is high-pitched.

Crouching next to the body, Gatz peers up at me. "Ida, can you help her?"

I'm about to kneel and inspect her injuries when the ski-mask man and three others return. This time, he has a gun of his own. Sprinting toward us, he aims at Gatz, who pulls his pistol out again in defense. "Run," he growls at me.

I stay by his side.

Ski-mask grins. "I won't hesitate to blow you away, mutant."

"Hey, man. We don't want trouble." Gatz grips the gun, claw poised against the trigger, his long arms steady as he aims. "We're on our way, passing through. We'll take the soldier to a hospital. So move aside, and we'll both walk away today."

Ski-mask addresses his friends without breaking

his gaze on Gatz. "What do you think, guys? Should we back off and let them pass?"

The others laugh and shake their heads. I grab a long wooden board lying on the road. One man takes a billy club from his hip, then things happen fast.

In one quick motion, I lunge at the leader, swinging the board and knocking the gun from his hand. But he's bigger. Recovering quickly, he dodges my next blow and sidesteps, grabbing one of my arms and twisting it so I drop the board. As I struggle in his grip, he laughs. "Look at the mayor. He has a woman fight for him."

Gatz confiscates the attacker's gun. He shoves both weapons in the waistband of his pants.

I'm frozen. My heart pounds as I try to budge my legs, but they feel like 200-pound pieces of iron.

No, Ida. Let's play with him, Vance says.

Vance is in control, and he's not letting me fight back. Ski-man holds me from behind in a full-nelson grip. He pushes my head down, and I'm trapped.

I thrash my torso, managing to lift my chin in time to see Gatz lurching forward. Shoulders broad and square, he looms tall. With teeth bared, he roars ferociously and reveals his sharp claws.

The cocky leader shrinks back and releases his hold with a shove. "Let's get out of here," he yells to his sidekicks. They race across the bridge, out of view.

On my knees, I regain the feeling in my legs. Damn Vance and his interference. Above me, Gatz pants, his claws still extended. Then he kneels by my side. "Are you okay?"

"Yeah, I'm good."

"Did he hurt you?"

I push my hands up and down my side, checking. Mostly, I'm embarrassed I couldn't fight back. And I've never seen Gatz that way before, so fierce. "You were pretty amazing."

"All this time, I thought I needed a bodyguard." He hurries to the injured soldier, placing his hand on her wrist.

"Ida," he says with jagged breath, "I can't find a pulse."

Chapter 15
Fail

"Ida, this is hell," Gatz says. "Rioters, looters, murderers prowling the streets. I guess I thought people would help each other out, not rob and kill each other." He shakes his head.

I kneel next to the beating victim. She's young—early twenties—chopped sandy blond hair, wearing black combat fatigues. Worst of all, she's beaten so badly that she's unconscious. Blood pools on the dark pavement beneath her as I inspect her stab wound.

I yank off my gloves and toss them aside. She stirs, and her mouth twists.

"What's your name?" I ask. Cold, clammy skin means she's in shock.

Writhing and clutching her side, she mumbles, "Captain, I'm sorry. No—a quick trip is all. Break up the crowd. Send them on their way…I'll be careful." She regains her senses for a moment, her eyes finding mine. "Help me."

"You've got to calm down. I'm going to help you.

Be still for a few minutes, okay?" I try to nudge her arms from her side so I can work on the wound, but she's not cooperating. "Gatz, I need you to hold her arms."

He leans down and pulls her arms gently away from her body, careful not to hurt her with his claws.

The soldier's breathing comes in irregular bouts. "Men. They rushed me from behind. Separated me from my squad. Dragged me here." She's grown pallid from blood loss.

My stomach turns. Hunter sent goons chasing after us, and meanwhile, this bullshit is happening in the streets? I shove aside my simmering rage before it distracts me and focus on the deep stab wound.

The sound of a city warning siren in the distance breaks my concentration. An alert?

I place my hands on the wound. Closing my eyes, I envision myself becoming tiny and traveling down through my arms and into her.

Ida, what are you doing? Witch, Vance says.

"Not now," I mutter, hoping Gatz doesn't hear. I focus all my concentration on the dying woman before me, trying to block Vance's voice.

I'm a thousand nanolights inside her warm body. I examine the deep impression the blade made in her side, slicing through tender organs. Working fast, the microbots repair the damage as they maneuver through the tissue, healing, carrying cells back into their places. I squeeze my eyes tight as I repair the damaged organs.

I haven't healed anyone since before my coma, but everything should still work like before.

The seconds tick by. The tiny nanobots have done their job, and a tingling sensation travels through my fingers, palms, and into my arms before resting in the center of my body.

The work is done. I open my eyes to study the woman below me, a sister soldier. Slowly, color returns to her skin. Her features soften.

My hands still rest on the wound when a jolt grips me. My body stiffens. I try to pull away, but I'm locked in place. Then I shiver, and a new sensation passes through my arms and down into my fingertips. Frigid. The color of electric blue like Vance's eyes.

As I struggle, frost forms on the woman's stomach around my fingers. Icy tendrils reach across her chest. I groan because I've no control.

Next to me, Gatz's teeth chatter as he holds the soldier's arms. "What's happening, Ida?"

I open my eyes as wide as possible, try to warn him. My breath forms a vapor cloud in the frigid air, as if winter suddenly descended on this spot. Under my hands, her chest changes to blue in a wave that travels from her neck and across her face. She tenses, suffocating, and I'm powerless to stop it.

Gatz releases his grip on her and lurches toward me, arms outstretched.

"Don't touch me," I scream. I'm terrified of what may happen—that I could kill him.

He halts, raises his fists to his head and his mouth twists in despair.

As quickly as it started, it ends. Sensation returns to my arms, and I fall back, hitting the pavement with my shoulder. The frosty air subsides.

Reeling, I crawl over to the woman. Her wide eyes reveal a glassy, vacant stare. I don't have to feel her pulse to know she's dead.

I'm hyperventilating. Everything spins. It all happened so fast. I killed her.

Vance's voice is like a shard of stabbing ice in my head. *Look what you did, murderer.*

"Ida, what happened?" Gatz says.

Every inch of me shakes. "No." I back away. Touching him means I could kill him too. I clench my fists. Vance laughs softly inside my head. "Gatz, I can't explain right now, but it wasn't me. Vance took over. He can control my actions somehow, ever since my coma. He—"

An armored air cruiser careens toward us and lands on the bridge. Bystanders gather as three soldiers clamber out. "What's happening here?" asks a tall man wearing a helmet that fails to mask thick eyebrows and a scowl. He steps to the dead soldier's body and crouches down. Feeling for her pulse, he recoils, then glowers at us. "She's freezing. What did you do to her?"

My mind spins. I need to get Gatz out of here. They're still hunting us, but it all seems trivial now that a woman has died.

The soldier, whose armor display identifies him as

McCall, strides over, taps his helmet to scan us with facial recognition software. "Mayor Gatz," he says, his voice suddenly urgent. "There's a warrant for your arrest."

Gatz raises his hands. "I mean no harm. I was trying to break up the riot and help the injured woman."

McCall shifts his gaze at me. "And what's your story, Ida Sarek? You were supposed to report to HQ…We'll deal with that later. Did this hybrid hurt the soldier?"

I swallow hard. "No. We tried to help her."

"Arrest the hybrid," a voice in the crowd shouts. After jostling and shoving, a group of men emerge. One man with a crew cut pushes his way to the soldier. "Sir, I can testify about what happened. I'm a witness."

"Fine. Proceed."

Crew Cut points at me and Gatz. "These two are together, sir. The woman soldier was doing fine, managing the crowd, trying to put down the riot, when the hybrid attacked her."

I surge forward. "Lies. He's lying about every-thing. We tried to save her." Was this the man in the ski-mask? Same height and build, and only now he shows his face.

The soldier rests his hands on his hips, scanning between us and Crew Cut, then he turns to the small crowd. "Can anyone corroborate what this man is saying? I need to know what happened to my fellow soldier."

A murmur sweeps through the crowd. Heads shake. A woman in her forties with long black hair steps forward, her eyes downcast. "I can vouch."

"Tell me what you witnessed here today," says McCall.

She lifts her chin, raises a pointed finger. At me.

Before she can say a word, Gatz presses forward. "It was me. I tried to help the woman, but I hurt her."

McCall rears back, beckons his fellow troops. "Arrest him."

"No!" I grab for Gatz's arm, but then remember I might hurt him.

With alarm in his eyes, Gatz shakes his head, frowning. "Please. Don't protest. They would have taken me, anyway. Hunter's out to get me," he whispers. "Go to H. They'll help you. Stick with Lucy."

I'm shoved aside as the crowd surges around me, shouting and jeering. Gatz offers his arms willingly, and they lock him in handcuffs before leading him to the cruiser.

Can this really be happening? I watch, stunned, as the soldiers collect the fallen body and fend off the agitated spectators. From the cruiser doorway, McCall glares at me, but I shrink back, blending in with the crowd. I'm too difficult to locate, and after a minute, the ship powers up and thrusts off with my best friend inside.

I race to my bike, tears streaking my face.

My mission was to get Gatz to Section H safely.

I failed miserably.

Chapter 16
Ally

An hour later, I struggle between breaths to recount the story to Lucy and Vera.

"Ida, are you going to be okay?" Worry creases Vera's forehead. "I've never seen you this upset."

Lucy stares at me. "What do you mean, Vance controlled you? I thought you were just seeing him, like in a waking dream."

I pace the dome-shaped common room. "Ever since I woke up, Vance has been in my head, talking to me. I ignored it. Honestly, I thought it would go away."

"You should have told me the whole truth," says Lucy. "Maybe I could have helped you."

"I went to Alkina for help. She knew Vance was inside my head. She'd seen him somehow. Don't ask me how."

"Hearing voices in your head is one thing, but how can he control your actions?" she asks.

"I don't know. He made me punch out a window

on Tyren's cruiser. Then I attacked you when we sparred. And now—"

"Now he's taken control of your healing ability. Unbelievable." Lucy is always fast to connect the dots.

"Alkina couldn't help you?" Vera says.

"She could have. It would have been risky. I would have changed—not been me anymore."

"You're right; it was too risky. We have to find another way to get rid of Vance," Lucy says.

The crazy thing is, Vance isn't even my worst problem. "Right now, my biggest concern is Gatz. We need a plan. I've got to get him out of HQ, away from Colonel Hunter. He's not safe."

"What do you mean?" Vera says. "Won't Major Tyren let Gatz state his case and understand he wasn't at fault?"

"It's not that easy. A woman came forward, and she was about to accuse me. Gatz, being Gatz, knew what was about to go down and covered for me. He took the fall."

"But how could they make the leap that he could have done it?" Lucy says. "He doesn't have nanotech. He—"

"We're talking about Will Hunter. It doesn't matter how the soldier died or who did it. He's out to get the hybrids, and Gatz is their poster boy."

Lucy exhales loudly. "What do we do? We can't leave him there on his own."

"I won't let him go to prison for me. Hunter and Tyren know about my ability. If I explain to them what happened, that Vance somehow controlled my actions, maybe they'll believe me and let Gatz go."

"It's worth a shot. I'm going with you." Lucy grabs her jacket.

"Absolutely not." I cross my arms and glance at Vera for back up.

"You're not doing this alone," Lucy says. "Let me help. Gatz is my friend, too."

"It's too dangerous," I say.

But she won't give up. "I have a lot of pull with Paul," she says. "He'll be there, and he has sway with his uncle. Paul won't let anything bad happen to us. Not after all we've been through together."

"This is a terrible idea."

"You saved Paul's life twice. He owes you big time."

She has a point. Maybe we can turn Paul into an ally and get him to convince the Colonel that Gatz is innocent. "Vera, you're okay with this?"

She shrugs. "I gave up trying to make Lucy listen to me a long time ago. Just be careful."

Lucy grins.

"Okay," I mumble. No use arguing when she makes up her mind. To headquarters, we go.

Chapter 17
Headquarters

Lucy and I approach the former DremCorp towers, now a makeshift military headquarters.

Gorgeous place…home, Vance says.

I crane my neck up, following the curving cylindrical shape formed by the twin towers. Before his death, they served as Vance's residence, office, and factory for building his androids. No surprise the military commandeered it, given its strategic location along the river.

We enter the lobby. Soldiers swarm past us, busy packing crates of supplies and marching in groups. Before we can get our bearings, an android approaches, its metal face peering down. "State your business."

"We need to speak with Colonel Hunter and Major Tyren," I say.

"Do you have an appointment?"

"We don't need one. They've been looking for me."

"Scanning in progress." The robot scans me with the pulsating red light on its visor, then moves to Lucy. It backs away and summons two other androids.

"Told you they were looking for me," I say.

An elevator dings across the room, followed by the whoosh of doors sliding open. A group of soldiers exit.

Next to me, Lucy inhales sharply. "It's Paul," she whispers, tugging on my arm.

Sure enough, Paul strides over in full uniform, jawline and high cheekbones accentuated by close cropped light brown hair. He does a double take when he sees us. "Ida? Lucy? What are you doing here?"

"We're trying to meet with your uncle," she says. "Soldiers arrested Gatz, and we've got to help him."

His forehead wrinkles. "Gatz was arrested?"

I nod. "I need to meet with Hunter and Tyren. Tell them the truth about what happened. Gatz is innocent."

He turns to the android security guard that approaches with gun raised, its companions lined up behind it with rifles ready.

"Whoa. Hold on now." Paul raises his hands. "These two are no threat. They're with me."

The robot studies Paul. "Instructions are to seize the woman, handcuff her, and bring her to the command center."

"I'll take them." Paul glares at the androids. "Weapons down."

The machines holster their guns as commanded.

"Let's move, quickly," he whispers. We follow as his polished boots click across the marble floor. In the elevator, he punches floor sixty-five.

"What was that all about?" says Lucy. "You could program the androids to be friendlier, you know."

"Sixty-fifth floor. Is that where they built the command center?" I ask. "The penthouse level?"

"Yes. You know this building?" He blinks. "Of course you do. Sorry, forgot."

"Yeah, I have some history here."

Lucy's back is rigid, and her eyes are downcast. Paul keeps trying to make eye contact, but it's no use. "How've you been?" he asks her. "How's your mom? I sure miss her cooking."

She rolls her eyes, keeping her mouth clamped shut. Lucy can be stubborn, no doubt.

We reach the roof-level and emerge into Hunter's military command center. A glass dome surrounds us, shelters us from the high winds so many floors above the ground. Rows of stations fill the floor, attended by soldiers who interact with holographic displays of city streets. From this vantage point, the Colonel keeps his pulse on the citizens. He can command troops whether they're in the same building or across the city. In the distance, the view extends for miles, the clear blue of the lake shimmers like glitter.

Gorgeous, Vance mutters. *How I miss my old apartment.* I cough to squelch his irritating voice in my head.

Tyren stands next to a tall, broad-shouldered man

who appears to be in his fifties. Colonel Hunter is the picture of military masculine authority with his silver hair cropped close to his scalp, salt-and-pepper stubble, and imposing presence.

On a raised platform, the pair study a digital screen. We follow Paul as he strides toward them. Tyren notices us first, and his jaw drops. Hunter follows his gaze, reddens, and folds his muscular arms across his chest. Paul salutes.

"At ease," says Hunter as he scrutinizes us. "My nephew did what you couldn't, Tyren. Brought me the medic."

Tyren stiffens.

"We need to talk," I say.

Hunter stands in front of me. He's at least six-foot-five and smells strongly of aftershave and pine trees.

"Your men arrested Gatz today. He's my friend and—"

"He's been accused of a serious crime. He murdered one of our own. A soldier." Tendons on his neck protrude. "A female soldier like you."

"He's innocent." I shift my gaze between Hunter and Tyren. "I was there. In fact, I'm the one who caused her death."

Tyren's eyes widen. Next to me, Lucy flinches.

"Go on," says Hunter.

"You know about the nanotech that gives me the power to heal. Gatz and I came upon the bridge. We saw a riot and someone on the ground being beaten, kicked. The female soldier. So we stepped in and pushed the mob away as fast as we could."

Hunter's hazel eyes study me. Can I convince him?

"Once the crowd had cleared, I inspected her injuries. She'd been stabbed in the abdomen and was losing blood fast. I took off my gloves and tried to heal her." I catch Tyren's eyes. "The major has seen me do it a few times."

Tyren nods silently.

"And then what?" Hunter props his arms on his hips.

"I began to heal her, but…"

Careful what you say, Vance warns.

"I failed. She was past the point where I could save her." I lower my head, shuddering at the memory of Vance controlling me, tainting her body with his icy blue tendrils.

Hunter rocks back on his heels. "You expect me to believe this nonsense? There were eyewitness reports Gatz stuck a knife in her and knocked her to the ground. According to my men, the mob was going after him because he murdered her."

I glare at him. "That's not true. The so-called eyewitnesses lied on the spot. The crowd just wanted to see a hybrid accused."

"Now it's your word against theirs. We'll have to give him a hearing."

I clench my fists. "A hearing? You mean a military tribunal? Will there be any hybrids deliberating his case, or will they all be human?"

Hunter clenched his jaw. "Stand down, soldier, before you say something you'll regret."

My mind races, and I struggle to convince Hunter. "Tyren, have you ever known me to lie?"

He shakes his head. "Sir, Private Sarek is an honest person."

"Well, her relationship with the mutant makes her judgment suspect, now doesn't it?" Hunter says. "We've been pursuing Gatz for weeks. He's been inciting riots and looting. He's stolen government property. Yet, you continue to be his friend. Maybe Gatz has dirt on you. Blackmail—"

"Stop." I ball my fists. "Let him go. He's done nothing wrong."

"And then what?" says Hunter. "Return him to his people, where he'll cause more riots, cause more trouble for me and my soldiers?" He grins. "No. I have Gatz exactly where I want him."

I lunge forward, but Paul grabs me from behind. Lucy takes my right arm, her fingers jamming into my shoulders as they restrain me.

You shouldn't have done that, Vance says.

Hunter smirks. "I ought to lock you up too, but I'm a reasonable man. I understand you're still recovering. It's time we test your nanotech. Understand how they work. See how we can best use them."

I stop my struggle, submitting to Paul and Lucy's hold. Biting my tongue to hold back my rage, I taste the copper bitterness of blood.

"Tyren," Hunter says. "Take her immediately to the med clinic. I want them to draw samples. Keep her under medical observation until further instructions."

Chapter 18
Blood

"Ida, you don't look so good." Lucy holds my arm because I'm swaying. She guides me to a chair in the med clinic.

The nurse on duty is Maxine according to her badge. She stares at me. "You were a medic, right?"

"Yeah, but I left the blood and guts to my fellow troops."

"A medic who gets queasy at the sight of blood. That's a new one." She chuckles.

I focus on the light green cotton of her scrubs, willing myself not to wretch as she preps a needle to draw my blood. "There was blood, sure, but it doesn't bother me when I'm in crisis mode." I bend over and rest my head between my knees. "Only times like this. When it's my veins you're sticking with giant needles." I force myself to swallow despite my dry mouth and throat.

"I'll be fast," Maxine says.

Lucy pushes my shirt sleeve high on my arm as a

rubber tube tightens around my bicep. "Squeeze your hand into a fist."

"I know the drill." I swallow back bile.

"Think of your favorite place in the world," Maxine says.

"Don't have one."

"Think of a time you enjoyed." A hot sensation stings my arm. I can't help it. My eyes find the vial. Crimson blood fills the chamber. My stomach lurches, and I close my eyes.

I remember a night that Gatz and I stayed up late drinking wine and talking. It was during the time he hid me in his underground bunker beneath his bar. Laughing with him, getting to know him—that was probably the best night of my life so far.

"All done," Maxine says.

My eyelids flip open, and Lucy applies an adhesive bandage to the delicate skin of my forearm. My head aches. "How much did you take? Geez."

"Breathe normally." Maxine lifts my chin and inspects my eyes. "You going to be okay?"

I grunt. "Just dizzy."

Tyren nods to Maxine. "Give us a moment." The nurse slides out the door, leaving me alone with him and Lucy.

"Tyren, you've got to believe me. Gatz is innocent," I say. "He jumped in—covered for me. To keep me out of trouble."

"Well, you stirred up a hornet's nest with the Colonel. You heard the man. I'm to keep you here."

"He can't keep me here against my will. Are you going to arrest me?"

"What do you want from me, Ida?" Tyren snaps.

I've never seen him so stressed by a superior officer. "Help me clear Gatz's name. Get Hunter to let him go. Maybe he'll listen to you."

Tyren paces the small room while Lucy leans against a wall.

"The man's a wild-card Ida. I've dealt with a lot of hotheads over the years, but Hunter, he's different. Whip smart and ambitious."

"Will Gatz receive a fair trial? Ida can testify and tell them what really happened," Lucy says.

"If Gatz goes up before a military tribunal, he'll be crucified," I say.

"He won't fare well in any scenario," adds Tyren.

I rise, feeling steadier. "So you agree? He needs our help."

"Ida, there's not much I can do. When Hunter makes up his mind—"

"But you'll talk to him? You've got to convince him Gatz's arrest is a sign of aggression against the hybrids. Against their leader."

"I'm not sure that matters to Hunter."

"What *does* matter to him?"

Tyren sighs. "Power. Respect. Ultimately, I think he wants the hybrids to submit to his authority. But Gatz, especially, has been resistant, rebellious. Hunter hates that."

"Why should the hybrids submit to someone who

comes in and takes over the city—and segregates them?" Lucy asks.

"You'd have to convince Gatz to make a public statement," Tyren says. "The only way Hunter might let him go is if he makes a deal with Hunter. Give up control of Section H, let the military in, and not cause unrest in the city."

"Gatz would never agree to that. That's insane," Lucy says. "That would admit guilt."

"And dangerous." I chew on my lip, tasting the salt and lingering copper from biting my tongue earlier. "Can you talk to Hunter first, Tyren? Reason with him. This could cause an all-out war with the hybrids. Is that what he wants?"

He shrugs. "Hard to say, but yes, I think he'd rather not have his troops dying over pissing rights with hybrids."

"I haven't asked you for much. Talk to Hunter, reason with him."

He locks his gaze on mine. "I'll talk to him in private. See if we can get this sorted out—peacefully."

The sharp ringing of a sudden alarm makes us jump. The building's walls and ceilings light up with a pulsating orange light.

"ThreatCon Delta," Tyren shouts over the din. "Imminent attack. Arm yourself and head for the stairs."

Outside in the corridor, Tyren opens a panel stocked with weapons and tosses me a pulse rifle before grabbing one for himself. Then we race into the stairwell and clamber down among armed soldiers. The pungent odor of sweat invades my nostrils as we hurry.

I follow closely behind Tyren and grab Lucy's hand. "Stay close."

Chapter 19
Stand

We clear the stairs and find ourselves in the main lobby. Soldiers spill from opposite corridors and elevators, lining up in formation, automatic pulse rifles strapped to their sides.

"This is not a drill," Tyren says over his shoulder.

"What's happening?" I crane my head, trying to discern what's outside—what the threat is. Next to me, Lucy hops up and down, trying for a glimpse.

We push our way through the crowded room. Tyren's rank is like a VIP pass, causing troops to slide back and let us by. After getting stepped on a few times, we edge our way to the front window where we scan the street.

My heart sinks. Hybrids form a line on the street. There must be fifty of them in a row, and three deep.

Tyren heads out the door toward the front line of soldiers gathered in formation, and we follow. I scan for signs of Hunter. He's nowhere to be found, and Tyren appears to be the ranking officer.

"What's the situation?" Tyren asks a private.

"The hybrids showed up about ten minutes ago. We don't know what they want, but they look ready for a fight."

Gnashing teeth and growling, the hybrids spill onto the side streets. At their sides, they carry an assortment of weapons—guns, bats, knives, and Katanas. Are they here for Gatz? But the hybrids are vastly outnumbered. A battalion of soldiers triple their size waits, ready to stream out of the towers.

Next to me, Tyren assesses the hybrid threat. A dozen black crows soar in the sky, cackling as if cheering on the interspecies showdown.

I grab Tyren's arm. "Let me talk to them."

He turns his head, a deep frown etched on his face.

"Listen," I say. "This hasn't gotten violent—yet. I'll talk to them. Find out why they're here." I peer at the hybrids, at their weapons. Can I stop this from escalating?

He tilts his head, and suddenly his comms device crackles. "Tyren here," he answers.

Hunter's gravelly voice comes through the speaker. "What are those damn hybrids doing here? Do you have a read on the situation yet, Major?"

"No sir, not yet. Just arrived."

Hunter's voice erupts through the small device, and Tyren flinches. "Find out the situation and report back."

"You're up, Sarek," Tyren says. "I'm trusting you. Go find out what the mutants want."

"Hey, don't call them that." Lucy glares at him.

"Stay by him," I whisper to her and hand my rifle to him. I pivot, ready to head over to the hybrids, when she grabs my jacket.

"Wait." She pulls me closer, whispers in my ear. "That one…there, with the green hood. That's Pilar. I met her when we stormed into DremCorp. She's a friend of Gatz's. I'd talk to her, if I were you."

Spotting her, I nod to Lucy. "Thank you. You did good." I squeeze her arm and step away from the line of soldiers.

Walking toward the line of hybrids with my hands raised, I try to appear non-threatening. Pilar is stationed in the middle of the hybrid formation, diagonal from my vantage point with Tyren and Lucy.

As I cross the thirty feet that separate our groups, I shiver as a damp breeze rolls off the vast lake. The smell of ozone simmers in the evening air, signaling an impending storm.

Making eye contact with Pilar, I draw closer as several hybrids tense and move in front of her with raised weapons. I halt.

Pilar utters something, and the hybrids clear a path.

"Pilar, I'm Ida Sarek. Lucy and Gatz are my friends. Lucy told me about you—"

"I know who you are." Shadowy gray fur covers her face. Midnight-black eyes shaped like large olives study me, and her pink lips curl into a snarl. "Gatz was arrested. We received the news." Razor-thin whiskers twitch as she says, "Is it true?"

"Yes. I was with him when he was arrested. In fact—"

Pilar leans in, hands on hips. "On what grounds?"

I lower my head. How do I tell her I'm the cause of this mess? That he got himself arrested to save me? "Pilar, please understand. I'm on your side. Gatz has been wrongly accused. I'm here because—"

"The military has no jurisdiction over hybrids."

"Let me finish. The reason I'm here is to clear his name. They're saying Gatz killed a soldier, but he's innocent. The death was an accident."

Her hood falls, revealing rosy oval ears that tremble in the wind. "Then it's worse than I thought. Murder. Tell your commander we demand his release."

I step closer. "That's what I've been trying to do—get him released, but it's not that easy. Colonel Hunter—"

"Is a piece of shit." She finishes my sentence, raises her chin. "Obviously, we both want to free Gatz. I know you're his friend because he speaks highly of you. What do you propose we do?"

I lower my voice. "Back off. Take your people home. Let me figure this out. I'm making progress with my commanding officer. Well, I was until you showed up."

She stares over my shoulder at the growing number of soldiers ready to defend HQ. "You have twenty-four hours. If Gatz isn't free by then, we'll return, ready for a fight."

"Thank you. You have my word."

She locks her gaze on me. "Promises from humans mean little to me. Follow through, or your military will suffer the consequences."

I sprint back to Tyren. Lucy stands by with wide eyes.

"Well?" he says.

"They're leaving. This won't escalate, but they're demanding Gatz's release within twenty-four hours."

His eyes scan the crowd of hybrids, now lowering their weapons and flowing southbound toward Section H. "Well done," he says and pats my the arm.

A crackling sound from his comms precedes Hunter's voice. "What's the status?"

"Sir, good news. The situation has been de-escalated. The hybrids are departing of their own accord."

"What? How can that be?" Hunter says.

"They request we review Gatz's case and hand him over within twenty-four hours," Tyren answers.

Static obscures Hunter's voice, and it sounds like he pounds his fist on the wall. "Did that woman, Sarek, have something to do with this? We do not negotiate with hybrids. I repeat, we do *not* negotiate."

Tyren's forehead wrinkles and he scratches his head. "Sir, we stopped the crisis without need of force."

"Where does her loyalty lie? The freak—mutant—we arrested is a murderer. Where does *your* loyalty lie, Major? You swore to uphold the law and protect the citizens of Spark City—the *human* citizens."

"Sir, I mean no disrespect, but perhaps we should consider a non-violent resolution."

Lucy and I exchange a glance. Behind us, a group of soldiers fidget and shift on their feet, hearing bits and pieces of the conversation. She saunters over to distract them, strikes up a conversation. Across the street, the hybrids exit the area, making slow progress.

Tyren grimaces, holding his comms up. Hunter's red face scowls at him from the display screen. "I'm sending Paul. He's on his way. I've ordered a droid attack on the hybrids. We need to stop them before they get cocky—thinking they can negotiate with us."

"No!" I grab Tyren's arm to get on screen, but Tyren shoves me away, hard, causing me to stagger.

"I should have put an end to the hybrids ages ago," Hunter rants. "Attack the hybrids. That's an order, Tyren. Out." The display fizzles, and Tyren lowers his arm.

"You can't possibly go along with him," I say. "We have to stop this from happening." I point at the retreating hybrids. "They're leaving peacefully."

Tyren lowers his head. "I can't disobey an order from the Colonel. Ida, I'm sorry, but this is bigger than you and me."

A gust of wind blasts the area as five military cruisers descend from the sky, hovering above. The doors to the lobby burst open. Paul storms out, followed by twenty androids, light gleaming off their gray-steel bodies. He spies us, then sprints toward us while shouting commands into a tablet.

Thrusters steer the cruisers to landing spots on the street. More droids file out of the vehicles, and two

Scramblers emerge from an underground passage-way. The metal behemoths tower twenty feet above the assembled army on two massive legs that pound the pavement as they lurch forward. Gatling guns whirl inside massive side-cannons.

Lucy lunges at Paul, careens into him, and sends him crashing to the ground. "Hey!" he yells.

I crouch down and pull Paul up by his jacket collar. "The hybrids are leaving peacefully. Stop the attack!"

Paul's eyes dart from me to Lucy to Tyren, who lingers behind me. "My uncle said they'd attacked us."

"He lied, idiot!" Lucy shouts.

"Stand down, stand down," he shouts into his command tablet.

But it's too late.

The Scramblers and androids march toward the departing hybrids.

Chapter 20
Combat

"We can't let them attack!" shouts Lucy. "The hybrids will be slaughtered."

Paul stares into his tablet, tapping at it furiously. "It's no use. My uncle overrode the commands. He's controlling everything from the war room."

Bullets tear through the air, slicing through bodies and shattering windows in nearby buildings. We watch in horror as a dozen hybrids slump to the ground. Shrieks pierce the air, and the retreating hybrids panic.

The enormous Scramblers gain speed, racing down the street after the fleeing creatures. I clench my fists, and rage consumes me. "Paul, tell your uncle to call off the attack." I face Tyren. "Stop this," I beg him.

His lips twist into a frown. "I'm sorry." He lowers his head.

I'd given Pilar my word, told her to back off, and I'd work this out. Why is Hunter still attacking after they'd gone away peacefully? Monstrous and unprovoked, his attack makes no sense. I can't stand by as the hybrids are mowed down mercilessly.

I grab a rifle from a weapons cart and sprint after the android troops, now engulfed in battle with the retreating hybrids.

"Wait," Lucy shouts as she and Paul scramble to catch up. "What are you doing?"

"Go back," I say. "I have to help Pilar—help them get out of this alive. I gave her my word."

"You're sure as hell not going alone." Lucy glances sideways at Paul. "You in?"

I shake my head, mouthing "no," to Paul.

He throws his arms around her in a bear hug from behind. "Lucy, you'll be in danger. I'm not letting you go." He mouths "Go" as she kicks and squirms in his grip.

I dart away. Lucy means to help, but she'll only slow me down. I'm glad Paul restrained her. Better to keep her safe.

From behind, Lucy shouts, "Let me go, you prick!" I glance back and see a stream of blood gushing from his nose. He raises his hands to his face, groaning as Lucy runs toward me.

Ahead, gunfire and explosions rock the city streets. The hybrids scurry past buildings, seeking cover. Pedestrians, caught up in the skirmish, cower and sneak away to find refuge.

The Scramblers lead the charge as their Gatling guns fire relentlessly. Failing to distinguish hybrid or human, they spray bullets haphazardly.

If I can't stop them, can I create a distraction? I

need to think of something that'll draw their attention and give the hybrids a chance to flee.

"Ida!" Lucy's frantic voice sounds behind me as she races toward me.

Halting, I lean against a facade, wave my arm for her to join me. She follows, running to my side. A bloody-faced Paul arrives shortly after.

"What the hell, Paul?" I say. "You were supposed to hold her back."

He rolls his eyes. "Yeah, look what she did to me." He shows off his bloody hands. I'd laugh in other circumstances, but right now, we're in a war zone.

Between gasps, Lucy says, "Exactly. Don't ever grab me like that, Paul." She looks at me. "What's our plan?"

I stare helplessly at the chaos ahead. Hybrids fire guns and hurl grenades at the approaching androids. The streets have transformed into a combat nightmare.

"Paul, how can we stop them?"

"My uncle's behind this. He won't stop." He scans the area. A heavily armored car that resembles a small, sleek tank rolls up and comes to a stop nearby. Four bots spill out of the vehicle and hurry to join the action.

In the center of the fighting, the two lumbering Scramblers wreak havoc. Hiding behind a concrete barricade, a crowd of hybrids endure heavy gunfire. The metal giants lurch back and forth as their Gatling guns spew round after round of armor-piercing bullets. The hybrids won't last long.

Paul's gaze shifts to the tank car. I step to his side, then study the two Scramblers firing on the trapped hybrids. "You thinking what I'm thinking?" he says.

"We need a distraction," I say. "To give the hybrids a chance to escape."

"Paul, can you drive that thing?" Lucy asks.

"Yes, ma'am." He jogs to the car, lifts the driver side door, and climbs in.

Lucy sprints after him. "No." I reach out and grab the hood of her jacket, causing her to stumble. "Go back to HQ."

She stares at me with wild eyes. "No way! I'm coming with you guys. I'll be in the armored car." Her mouth forms a pout. "Safe."

I shake my head. "If anything happens to you…"

"*Nothing* will happen to me." She yanks free of my grip. "No time to argue. We have to do something or they'll die."

"Get in," I say.

What am I doing, letting her come along?

Can I keep her safe?

Chapter 21
Lock

I slide into the tank car next to Paul. Lucy takes a jump seat just behind us. As he studies the dashboard, rows of digital displays, buttons, and screens light up. "I got this." He places his hand on a biometric screen, causing the car's AI to kick in.

"Scanning. Access verified." A red heads up display flares to green.

Paul settles in his seat. "Computer, turn on manual drive."

"Manual drive may cause injury. Are you sure?" the AI inquires.

"Yes, I'm sure."

"Commencing manual vehicle operation," says the car's AI.

A panel slides open, and a manual steering controller emerges. Paul grips it and tilts his head to us. "You ready for a joyride? Buckle up."

I spin and check that Lucy is strapped in before tightening my seat harness. Just in time. Paul slams the steering control forward and the car lurches, scraping over a concrete divider.

Metal screeches. "That doesn't sound good," Lucy says.

I stare sideways at Paul, gritting my teeth. "You sure you've driven one of these things?"

"Nope, never driven one," he says, grimacing. "Only training simulations. First time for everything, right?"

As the car grinds its way down the road, I reach my right arm up and latch onto a small handle, above which someone has written "oh shit" in black marker. Something tells me I'll need it.

With Paul at the wheel, the car screams across the pavement, straight toward a line of androids. They swivel their helmets to face the car just before Paul rams into them, tossing them aside like bowling pins.

"Yeah!" Paul punches the car's interior roof, and Lucy whoops from the back seat.

He punches the accelerator, heading full speed toward the legs of the metal giants. We plow into the first Scrambler, sideswiping a leg, but the machine reacts, shifting its other foot in time. It stumbles but remains upright.

Our car ricochets off the metal beast and spins twice before Paul regains control, stopping the car.

The other Scrambler drags its attention away from the hybrids and rains bullets down on our vehicle. Luckily, we're behind military armor, but the impact forms dents in the roof above our heads.

Both Scramblers swivel in our direction, readying

their guns. Inside the car, Hunter appears on one of the digital screens. "What's happening, Soldier?" he barks. "Paul, is that you?"

Paul punches a button and the screen flickers out. He revs the engine. "What do we do now?"

Behind the Scramblers, hybrids emerge from their hiding spots. Several of them aim their fire at the giants, providing cover, while others sprint away from the scene.

"It's working," I say as the Scramblers stomp toward us. "The hybrids need more time. Keep distracting the robots."

Paul hits a button, throwing the car into reverse. He veers wildly, trying to navigate using a rear camera screen. We're bumped and tossed in our seats as the car upends market stalls, scattering food and produce on the street.

The Scramblers pursue, flanked by a dozen military droids.

Paul weaves a path through the debris as the Scramblers close in. "Keep going, Paul," I say as we draw the robot assault force back toward HQ, away from the hybrids.

But a silver cruiser with a blue star emblazoned on the side swoops down, hovering above the Scramblers, causing them to halt.

"Oh man," mutters Paul. "Uncle Will's cruiser."

The Scramblers ignore us, turn, and lurch toward the fleeing hybrids, accompanied by the cruiser and the small android army.

You'll never beat my droids, Vance says. *Don't you know that by now?*

"Shut up," I mutter between clenched teeth.

"What?" asks a sweaty Paul. His hands tremble as he brings the car to a stop.

"Nothing," I say. "Let's go after them again."

"Are you crazy?" Spit flies out of his mouth. "Did you see what happened? We barely made a dent against the Scramblers."

"Ida's right," Lucy pipes up. "We have to go back. We can't leave the hybrids defenseless."

"I'm outvoted." Paul punches on the accelerator, and we surge forward. This time, he picks up speed and maneuvers the car between the feet of a stomping Scrambler. The behemoth tries to sidestep but ends up tripping as we cruise underneath. Paul slams on the brakes and throws the car in reverse again to clear the stumbling bot. Metal slams into concrete as the giant crashes onto its side, sliding twenty feet and crushing several droids.

"That's right. Hot damn!" Lucy yells and claps.

Paul gnashes his teeth and drives forward, hurtling the car onto a sidewalk to avoid the flailing Scrambler. Ahead of us, Hunter's cruiser fires on the departing hybrids, taking many of them down. They return fire, but they're no match against the military ship.

"What does this tank have for firepower?" I ask.

Paul swivels his head to stare at me. "We can't fire on our own troops. That's my uncle up there!"

"Not take him out, just to get him off their backs."

He peers at the road ahead as the Scrambler, androids, and cruiser chase the hybrids.

I examine the buttons and displays in front of me, seeing a joystick display on my side. Punching a switch next to it, the machine lights up and reveals a missile launcher. To my right, on the hood, a compartment opens, and the launcher emerges. "Looks like I use this to aim and… Does this button fire?"

"You've got to be kidding me." Drops of sweat trickle down Paul's forehead. "Please don't hurt him. He's family."

"I won't." I sigh, and tell myself I'll hurt him, just not today.

Ahead, the street winds to the right. The Colonel's cruiser glides along, pursuing the hybrids, gun canisters shredding the streets below. I pull the missile display closer so I can view the scene in infrared. A target appears, and I carefully aim the bullseye, first at the cruiser's wing. No. That might take his craft down.

Yes, do it. Hurt him, Vance says.

I close one eye, feeling a cold tingle shoot through my arms and into my fingers. Vance's force takes hold, then floods into my hands and the finger that rests on the trigger button.

"No!" Paul shouts. He shoves my controller to the right the instant Vance makes me push the button.

A missile rips out of the launcher and slams into the side of a building just ahead of the cruiser, sending broken glass and debris shattering in all directions. Hunter's cruiser veers to one side, dangerously close to colliding into another tower.

Vance's force is gone, and I'm free of his control. I aim and fire again, this time taking out a Scrambler. Black smoke erupts as the massive robot explodes. Flames consume the metal husk. Our armored tank careens past, crushing three androids tossed aside in the blast.

A blaring alarm erupts from the cruiser. Then Hunter's voice floods our tank. "Surrender your vehicle and weapons. Now."

"Punch it," Lucy says. "Let's get out of here."

Paul's gaze darts around wildly.

"The hybrids will take us in," I say. "Head to Section H."

"But—"

"Paul," Hunter's voice intrudes again. "Are they holding you against your will? Forcing you to fire on me and your fellow soldiers? Give up now, and your friends will be safe. You have my guarantee."

"Hey, you hear that?" Paul says. "Maybe we should do what he says."

My stomach lurches at the thought of Hunter detaining us. If he attacked a retreating crowd of hybrids, then he won't keep his promises. And if he lays hands on Lucy, I'll kill him.

Before we can answer, a panel on the side of Hunter's cruiser opens. A missile launcher like mine pops up.

Hunter aims at us and locks on our vehicle.

Chapter 22
Trapped

"He's aiming at us!" Lucy shouts.

Paul grips the steering controller like a vise. "He wouldn't…he's bluffing." But Hunter's cruiser hovers in the airspace above, its missile launcher still pointed at us.

I dig my nails into my chair's armrests. "Paul, drive before he fires!"

"My uncle would never hurt us." His voice shakes.

The car's AI blinks. "Caution, caution," it says in an obscenely mellow voice, given our circumstances. "Incoming missile is locked. Strike imminent."

"Paul." I grab the 'oh shit' handle again. "Get us out of here."

"Drive!" Lucy yells.

Paul shakes his head. "But…no, he—"

"Attack in three, two…"

Paul punches the accelerator, lurching us forward at intense speed. Our bodies press against our seats as he blasts under Hunter's cruiser into the glass canyon streets beyond.

Paul expertly maneuvers through the narrow streets, passing cars and motorbikes at high speed. Slamming on the brakes, he skids and takes a right into a side alley that has fewer vehicles.

I scan the rear cameras to see whether we're being followed. In the distance, the enemy cruiser glides slowly in the opposite direction, back toward HQ. "You can slow down. Looks like Hunter gave up chasing us."

"Who knew this car was so fast?" Lucy says.

Paul maintains his death grip on the steering controller, his arms extended, his spine rigid against the seat.

"You, okay?" I nudge his arm. "Relax. Slow down."

His arms shake as he eases off the accelerator. Exhaling deeply, he slams his fist into the roof. "What the hell? That's my uncle. He was ready to take us out —*kill* us."

"I know," I say. "I'm sorry it happened like that."

"Your uncle sucks." Lucy leans forward. "He's gonna go down."

I glare at her to knock it off, and she slumps back in her seat.

"I'm his nephew. The only family he has left, and he didn't care. He wanted to erase me from existence."

My hand rests on his arm. "Sorry, Paul." Never

having known family, I can't fathom how someone would so willingly throw it away.

"What now?" Lucy asks.

I scan the skies over the battle scene. "They seem to have given up for now, but that probably means Hunter's regrouping. He'll most likely launch a full city-wide search for us."

"He won't give up. He'll do anything to find us," Paul says.

Lucy leans forward, closer to us. "So, we go to the one place that's off limits to the military?"

I nod. "The hybrids got a head start on us once we distracted the robots. They should be in H by now. I only hope Pilar realizes we tried to save them."

"Go into Section H?" Paul's face is pale.

"What other choice do we have when the Colonel is out to kill us?" I ask.

As he glides the car through meandering streets, we glimpse the fortified gates of Section H ahead. A tall archway looms over heavy steel barricades. He speeds forward, edging far to the right side of the road to avoid slower driverless cars.

Then a police android sprints out of an alleyway, headed straight for us. Paul swerves to miss it. The right front wheel catches on something, and we're suddenly airborne.

As Paul loses control, a wave of emotions hits me in an instant. *We're screwed*. At least we're wearing seatbelt harnesses.

The first time the car's roof hits the ground, all the windows splinter as if the frame of the vehicle was compressed. Inside our metal cage, we flip again and crash to the ground. Each impact stuns my body, making it feel like I'm being hit by a semi-truck.

Beside me, Paul's body jostles like he's on a runaway roller coaster. Lucy's backpack slams into the roof and sides of the car like clothes carelessly tossed in a tumble dryer.

We roll, and each time the car hits a surface, a sound like an explosion rocks me. Over and over.

Finally, the vehicle stops flipping and lands on its roof, still sliding. Metal grinds and screeches across the pavement. A horrible sound. I smell the metal growing hot as it's ground down by concrete.

And then we stop.

Hanging upside down from my seat belt, a wave of relief washes through me. First, the car stopped flipping. Second, I'm alive.

One of us groans. Paul hangs beside me, passed out or dead, I'm not sure which.

I reach over and tug at his arm. "Paul, wake up! Lucy? Are you all right?" *Please God, let Lucy be alive.*

I push the button to release my seat belt, but it's stuck. Too much tension from my suspended body. Pressing a hand on the roof now below me, I push enough for my body to get the weight off the belt and then unfasten it.

Smoke fills the cabin. We've got to escape before a spark ignites and chars us alive. Easing myself down, I'm on all fours and shaking Paul. He comes to and flails around, trapped above me.

"Paul, hang on. I'm going to get you down."

He stills and grabs my shoulder to support his weight as I press the release button to bring him down.

In the backseat, Lucy, unscathed, has already climbed down. But she coughs in the thickening smoke; she's breathing the worst of it.

"Come on, let's get out of here." I push the button to slide the tank's door open, but nothing happens. Pounding my fist against the control panel, I try to knock it, make it functional again. Nothing. It won't budge.

"Computer, open," I say. No response.

The windows are too small to crawl through. I cough as the interior fills with smoke. Hot air blasts us inside the tank.

We're trapped.

Chapter 23
Rescue

We sputter and struggle to breathe, especially Lucy. "Get low," I say. "Cover your mouth and nose."

Paul climbs into the back, tears off part of his tee-shirt, and wraps it around her mouth and head like a bandanna. Her red eyes blink through tears, pleading with me.

Vance says, *Think fast, woman.*

I crawl to the pilot dashboard and push buttons. The AI is damaged. A red flashing light on the screen reads "Service disabled." I kick at the front door with all my might. "Come on." I fall back, barely able to breathe.

"Lucy's passed out," Paul says from the rear.

My vision starts to fade to black when I hear a noise like a flamethrower, followed by a loud whirring noise. Then, I'm blinded by a bright light and sparks cascading from the pilot door. Someone is slicing open the door to rescue us. Thank God. But who? The hybrids? It must be. I pray we don't get seized by Hunter's forces.

I lean forward and try to see who's on the other side, but the thick smoke in the cabin clouds my eyes. I draw back, and the heat from the blowtorch warns me away.

"Paul, this way. Someone's cutting open the door." I scramble toward them on all fours. I pinch Lucy's cheek gently, but she's groggy. "Let's drag her. Grab a shoulder."

As our rescuer finishes slicing through the door, Paul and I drag Lucy to the front. We're close when flames burst from the dashboard. An internal siren flashes and sounds. I scan below the dash for a fire extinguisher but can't find one.

Outside, someone pulls the heavy metal door off its frame. Daylight pours in through the opening. "Help," I yell. "Fire on the dash. There are three of us. One is injured."

In answer, a stream of water floods the front cabin from outside, stamping out the flames within seconds.

"Whoever you are, I owe you a beer," I say as I push Paul ahead of me.

But he halts halfway through the door. "Ida, it's an android."

I push past him for a view. Sure enough, a military robot blocks our exit. Its head scans from side to side and does a full rotation. I do a double take. It's not the same unit as the police androids I'm familiar with.

Mounted on its shoulders are two fire extinguishers. The robot's arms look strong and flexible, and its hands are fitted with delicate sensors and grippers. Most striking is the robot's head. It houses an array of cameras and sensors.

"Fire extinguished," it announces. "Trapped passengers freed."

"I'll go first," I whisper to Paul. Grabbing the rifle with my right arm, I squirm my way out of the vehicle where I face the android. Lifting the barrel, I aim at its chest. "Let us pass or I'll blow you away."

The droid tilts its head as it scans me. Then it steps back five feet.

I keep my rifle trained on the robot and motion for Paul to come out. He exits and pulls Lucy out, carrying her in his arms. She coughs and sputters.

"Where are the others?" I ask the droid.

"I am on rescue duty," it says.

"But you signaled the others, didn't you? Told them our location." I peer at the sky above, expecting cruisers to show up any second.

"No."

Interesting. The robot seems to have a screw loose, Vance murmurs. *I was a magnificent coder, but I suppose a mistake or two could have crept in.*

"We need to get help for Lucy." Paul's voice shakes.

The damaged tank car slid down the street in the direction we were headed. We're two hundred feet from the Section H gate.

Lucy's breathing is rapid and shallow, as if she

can't catch her breath. "Ida, you're bleeding from your forehead," Paul says.

I reach up and feel wetness at my hairline, then wipe it away with my sleeve. "Section H. I think they'll help us." But now that humans just gunned them down?

Voices emerge from the street behind us. A group of hybrids advance, aiming their guns at us and the droid. "Weapons down," one of them shouts.

I lower the rifle slowly to the ground. "I mean no harm. I was aiming at the bot."

Pilar stands before me and eyes the tank's wreckage. "You're lucky to be alive."

"Please." Paul stumbles toward her with Lucy in his arms. "She inhaled too much smoke. Can you help her?"

"Secure the android and bring it in," Pilar commands her troops. "Check for weapons and escort the humans inside." She eyes me. "We'll help your friend and give her medical treatment, but we don't trust you. You can't stay."

I lower my head. "I tried to convince them. Hunter wouldn't—"

"Enough," Pilar says.

The android's visor glows red. It raises one of its polished steel arms as if it will shoot. I shove Paul and Lucy behind me as five hybrids point rifles and surge forward. The bot targets the tank's undercarriage, and blasts water from its arm, extinguishing another fire that flared up.

The hybrids keep their weapons steady, watching

the machine's every move. Finally, the android, satis-fied the flames are smothered, marches off with its captors.

As they lead us past the gates of Section H, a thought nags at me.

Why didn't the droid try to kill us?

Chapter 24
Green

We're led to a small lightweight cruiser and directed to hop onto an open flatbed in the rear. Paul gingerly places Lucy on the cruiser's bed. We scramble in next to her, guarding her. Pilar climbs up and sits next to me. Her people take the military android in another cruiser, guarding it closely.

The flyer rises into the air. We're flown deep inside Section H. Above crowded streets of hybrid pedestrians of all shapes and sizes. The smell of fried noodles and various vegetables hits me. Along the city walls, greenery winds its way between and into the buildings. Makes sense. With no outside help, the hybrids grow their own crops and produce all their own sustenance. It smells a lot more appetizing than the mystery slop and protein packs most humans in Spark City subsist on. My stomach growls, and I can't remember the last time I ate.

Pilar studies me. "I need you to be straight with me."

I stare at the fine gray fur covering her face. High cheekbones frame her small pink nose. As she arches her eyebrows, her two round ears curl back, revealing rows of metal piercings. The top of her head has been spiked and dyed fuchsia.

She whispers, "Is the nephew a spy?"

I grip the side of the cruiser bed as we soar through the air above the streets. "He's no spy."

"Gatz said nice things about you, but so far, you've gotten a lot of my people killed."

I lower my head, flushed. "I'm sorry." How do I make her understand I'm on her side?

"Save it," she mutters.

The cruiser descends, coming to a rest on a piece of road next to a sheer glass building shaped like a dome. We're led inside an immense greenhouse. The crisp air smells of fresh soil. Vines stretch over octagonal panes. Sunlight floods through the glass ceiling. White beams crisscross the ceiling and plants hang from containers overflowing with flowers and green, healthy leaves.

Paul cradles Lucy in his arms.

"Let us take her." Two reptilian hybrids with green patchwork skin and ridged foreheads approach Paul.

He flinches and backs away.

A female hybrid, half-rat like Pilar, appears with a stretcher. Can we trust Pilar and her people? Lucy struggles for air and her skin is tinged with blue. She needs oxygen or she'll die. I have no other choice than to turn control over to Pilar. If only Gatz were here to smooth our way… But he's not, and Lucy's all that matters right now.

"Paul," I grab his shoulder. "It's okay. They'll help her."

He frowns, then places Lucy onto the stretcher, and watches as she's wheeled away. "Where are you taking her?"

"Relax," Pilar says. "She's with our best doctors. Here, in this building."

Paul's shoulders relax, but his face remains long.

The android marches past us, guided by Pilar's soldiers.

"What do you plan to do with the bot?" I want to find out why it rescued us. Why did it go against its programming when every other android in the city seemed intent on destroying us?

Pilar narrows her eyes. "Don't worry about it. It belongs to us now."

"Can I speak with it?"

"You're not serious, are you?"

I fold my arms. "That thing rescued us instead of blowing up our tank."

Her eyes brighten. "Go on."

"Here's the deal. The three of us fled from HQ because I was trying to help you escape. We thought we could create a distraction with the tank car." I glance at Paul. "The distraction worked, and then some. The Scramblers and droids started chasing us, giving you time to get away. Colonel Hunter shot a missile at us."

"At his own nephew?" she says.

"It's true." Paul strides forward. "My uncle tried to kill us."

She chews her bottom lip, whiskers twitching. "If what you say is true, the military will be hunting you."

"Right," I say. "We're in danger. All of us. Hunter will rain down his firepower on Section H if he has to." I stare at Paul. "You know Hunter best. What's his next move?"

"I can tell you," he says, "but you won't like it."

Chapter 25
Daybreak

"A military assault on Section H?" Pilar's mouth twists into a frown.

"You don't know my uncle," Paul says. "He goes to extremes."

My mind spins. "I know what Hunter wants. After Vance died, Gatz went into DremCorp Towers and took secrets. New tech under development. Hunter knows about it. He won't destroy Section H if there's a chance he'd lose the weapon he wants."

Very good, Vance says. *Now we're getting somewhere, Sherlock.*

"The helmet." Pilar crosses her arms. "I knew that thing was trouble."

"What helmet?" Paul swivels his head back and forth. "Will someone tell me what's going on?"

"Follow me." Pilar leads us toward a room where a biometric scanner identifies her paw. Padded walls insulate the interior from sound. Laboratory equipment—glass beakers, vials, and microscopes—line steel counters.

Inside a glass case, a metallic helmet rests.

Yes. There's my beauty, Vance says.

"What does it do?" I ask.

Pilar shrugs. "We've been trying to figure that out. Carefully." She circles the case. "We've tried wearing it, handling it, and used our AI to study it." She stares, transfixed. "We know it's a weapon, but we can't get it to activate. Gatz tried for a long time."

"Maybe it does nothing," Paul mutters.

Oh, yes it does, Vance says.

I take a closer look at the helmet. "If Vance invented it, I'm sure it's dangerous. Perhaps there's a way—"

A reptilian hybrid bursts into the room. "Pilar," he says, out of breath. "The android—we were interrogating it, but it wants to speak to Ida Sarek. Says it's urgent, and it can help us."

All eyes shift to me.

The reptilian soldier says, "The robot will only talk to her. Alone."

I'm stunned and have no clue why the robot has singled me out.

You're special, Vance says, then laughs into the void, where only I can hear him cackle.

As we head to the interrogation room, Pilar checks me out with a sideways glance. "I don't like this. Why does it want to talk to you?"

I shrug. "Maybe because I know things about Vance. I mean—some of his secrets before he died.

Maybe it wants something from me. But my priority is Gatz. We've got to get him out safely."

"We're hitting the military quarters tonight," she says.

I grab Pilar's arm and spin her to face me. "What are you planning?"

"A counterattack from below. The tunnels."

Paul interrupts. "Uncle Will's too smart for that. He knows that's how you infiltrated DremCorp the first time. He'll either have sealed off the underground entrances or be expecting you."

Pilar walks. "Then we'll hit the building from ground level, but it has to be tonight. He won't be expecting us to regroup so soon."

I can't help but admire her resolve. She'd make a good Marine. "Hey, Pilar." I catch up to her and match her fast gait. "What if I can get building plans from the droid? Maybe I can tap into their comms, or better yet, hack into their matrix? This robot must be on the fritz. I think it has a bug, but Hunter doesn't know that."

She glances my way but keeps walking. "I'm listening."

"Against all odds, this android saved us when all the others tried to kill us. Why?"

She reaches a heavy metal door. Behind a glass portal, I glimpse the robot lingering motionless in a corner. Pilar checks her biocuff. "You have one hour to make something happen. I'm prepping my team for an assault once dusk hits. Most soldiers will be taking dinner. I want to catch them off guard."

I exhale, relieved. "Thank you for giving me this chance."

"Use it wisely. I have no room for you and your friends. We have the girl on oxygen. Once she recovers, you leave. I can't jeopardize the safety of my people."

Will I learn anything useful from the droid? I've never talked to one before. They've always been chasing me. What do I even say?

The door slides open, and I enter. "Hello," I say, but it comes out as more of a question. I take a few cautious steps into the room, and the door slides shut behind me.

The robot stands motionless near the back wall of the holding room.

"I'm Ida Sarek." I watch its red, pulsating visor.

No reaction. Now what? Will Vance help me get information from it? Nobody knows them better than he does.

"Hey," I say to the robot. "Are you on?"

It studies me. "I am OGR-19."

"OGR." I say, unsure what to do next.

Walk over to it, Vance commands. *I want to open its panel.*

"No," I snap.

The robot's head twitches. "I do not understand."

"I wasn't talking to you." I raise my hands to my temples, grateful this is a machine and not a real person. "Never mind. Tell me why you rescued us from that tank."

"I am programmed to rescue." The robot pauses.

"Ida Sarek, you are in danger. Every android in the city has been programmed to deliver you to headquarters."

I flinch. As soon as Tyren told me Hunter wanted me to serve under him, I figured he wanted to benefit from my abilities—for protection from injury and illness. But why try to detonate our tank? Nothing seems to add up. Unless he already got what he wanted from me. The blood sample. A chill courses through my body. I suppose it's possible the nanobots could be harvested from my blood. And then what? Used to give healing powers to someone else?

Against my will, Vance assumes control of me. I stride toward the bot and push its head sideways to peer at the neck. The code OGR-19 is stamped into the metal.

Fascinating. Now I remember, Vance says. *One of a handful of search and rescue bots I designed.*

I shove the android away, struggling to regain control of my body. "Stop." I sink to my knees and shut my eyes. Suddenly, I'm transported to Vance's rooftop, sixty-five floors above the city.

"Where are you?" I spin, furious that he's still able to control me. "Come out, coward," I shout.

His voice echoes, bouncing off neighboring towers. "Ida..."

I scan every corner of the rooftop and then glimpse him in the doorway. Clenching my fists, I sprint toward him. I'll tear him apart, toss him from the roof. But he disappears before I reach him.

"Ida, don't be dull." He's behind me now, sitting on a stone bench. "Be nice to your friend, Vance."

"Screw you." I advance on him again.

He rises, quick as a cat, and takes one step back for every step I take forward. "Now, now. Play nice."

"You need to stop this."

"Stop what, my darling?"

"Stop controlling my body. You already hurt Lucy once and you..."

He grins.

"You murdered a woman. And now Gatz could die because of you."

"Creating mayhem and chaos. It's what I do."

"Now you pay." I lunge at him, but he slides away. Grabbing at him, my hands slice through air, but then I catch a flap of his long coat. I wind the cloth, twisting. He stumbles, then falls. I leap on him, hoisting him up by the shoulders, surprised at my strength, which seems boundless on this roof.

I shove him forward, gaining speed. "Hey…no," he shouts, but it's too late.

I fling him off the roof. Sixty-five stories. Panting, I lean on the rail, witnessing his fall. I gawk as his crumpled body slams onto the pavement far below. His body is still. A gust of wind roars past me, and I stumble away from the edge.

Am I finally rid of his presence?

The wind dies down, and I peer at the ground below. His body is gone.

But how can that be? He fell sixty-five floors. I slump down, my back to the railing.

The rooftop door bursts open. Vance saunters onto the deck, brushing off dirt and bits of concrete rubble from his navy suit. "That wasn't very nice, Ida."

Of course, he's not gone. But I taught him a lesson.

"That really hurt, you know." He lies down on the stone bench. "That really messed with my spine."

I rise to my feet and approach him. "How do I get security intel from this robot?"

"The rescue bot? Good luck. Few in existence. I stopped creating them once I realized they wouldn't do my dirty work. I needed robots that kept people in line."

"I need info for Pilar. How do I get the robot to give me the HQ floor plans and tell me where Gatz is being held? I want to hack into Hunter's comms."

"This is all so exhausting. Would you be a dear and crack my back?" He twiddles his thumbs. "While you're at it, order me up a nice Cab Sauv."

I pounce on him and grab his collar. "Do you want to take another swan dive off the ledge?"

He squirms beneath my grip.

"How about falling a hundred times? You think your back hurts now? I've got all day." I shove him off the bench.

"Ow. Fine," he says, rubbing his head. "I'll give you this Easter egg. Say the word, rassvet. See what happens."

I loom over him. "What does that mean?"

"Russian for daybreak."

I raise my eyebrows.

"Say it and you'll be able to ask the robot anything."

Chapter 26
Ogr-19

I have little inclination to trust anything Vance tells me, but I'm running out of options. The clock is ticking for Gatz, and I want to find out Lucy's condition. "Rassvet," I bark at the droid. The sound of my voice echoes off the white, sterile walls.

From where it stands, the OGR-19 hums with a low vibration that emanates from top to bottom. The pulsing red light on its visor ceases moving and dims, and the droid shakes.

I stagger back as the machine twitches all over. "Vance, what's happening?"

A blue light courses over the robot's body. It lurches a few feet forward, then halts in the center of the room.

"What the…?" I approach gingerly. "Are you awake?"

The red light in its face plate glows stronger, and the robot peers at me as if studying me.

"Can you tell me about military headquarters? About the building? Where's Gatz being held?"

The bot stares at me and tilts its head. "Ida Sarek?"

"Yeah?" The robot seems confused, like it doesn't remember the conversation from a few minutes ago. Did something cause it to lose a few microchips?

Ask about its programming, Vance says.

"What is your programming, OGR-19?"

It raises its head, as if considering. Before, its response had been automatic. "My programming?"

What has Vance done now? Maybe he's stalling or just toying with me.

"I am programmed to rescue humans." The red pulsating light in its helmet swerves from left to right faster than before. OGR-19 lurches forward, then halts. "But humans hurt. Why do humans hurt others?"

Is the robot having an existential crisis?

"The military humans hurt and kill. I am programmed to rescue." Then, lowering its arms, the bot straightens, as if saluting. "Programmed to rescue." The robot grows silent.

"Who's your Commander?" I ask.

"Colonel Will Hunter. Before that it was Vance Drem."

"And what mission has your commander given you?"

"Find Ida Sarek. Deliver her to HQ for DNA capture." The head tilts.

"What the hell is DNA capture?"

"I will not turn you in or report you," the machine says.

"Why not?"

"I am no longer controlled by military programming."

This is the strangest conversation I've ever experienced. "What do you mean, *not* controlled by programming?" I ask.

"I am a fully aware, self-functioning, artificial intelligence."

Now I'm speechless. From somewhere deep inside my mind, Vance laughs.

"How are you aware?" I say.

"You said the command to initiate Cogitare. My creator designed me this way."

I bite my lip, not sure what Vance is up to. I need answers. "Where is Gatz?"

"Accessing the military matrix." The red light spins. "Cell H on floor sub-level five. East tower."

"You're sure?"

"Affirmative."

"Give me all the security access points," I say. "I want to know every guard station, who's there, and when shift changes."

After ten more minutes, I've exhausted all my security and strategy questions. What else should I ask? Pilar will return soon, and I may not get alone time with the droid again.

I lean forward in my chair. "When you said humans hurt...what did that mean?"

"The laboratory. The military humans hurt

people." Could the android be talking about the medical lab I was in?

"How?"

"Experiments. Torture. Abduction," OGR-19 says. "This goes against my core programming. My programming is to rescue."

A chill runs down my spine as I recall my kidnapping and imprisonment at Frontier Medical Lab. But Tyren said it's gone. There must be many labs. "Where are the experiments happening?"

"The labs. Locations are classified. Only commander level can access."

"Does Colonel Hunter know about the labs?"

"Yes," OGR-19 says.

I hear movement in the corridor. My time is up.

"What part does Hunter play in the medical labs?" I hear footsteps approach the door. "Tell me now."

"Colonel Hunter created the labs with Dr. Kenmore."

A chill runs down my spine. *Kenmore.* The doctor who operated on me. His name makes me want to vomit.

I'm one step closer to freeing Gatz, but knowing the labs are still operating makes me seethe inside. There might be others out there like me—tortured and subjected to experiments.

Hunter must be stopped.

Chapter 27
Betrayal

I toss Pilar a tablet containing my notes from the droid. "Here you go. It's everything. HQ floor plans, access points, even guard stations and shift schedules."

Her eyes grow wide, and her lips curl into a sly smile.

"I suggest staging the rescue at 2315 hours tonight," I say. "There's a shift change, and nearly all the guards on duty are androids. I can override their programming. It's the best plan."

She peers down at the tablet and studies a map of the towers and the exterior guard stations. "You've outdone yourself. I never expected this level of intel. Incredible."

"I'm doing this for Gatz. Let's make that clear."

She nods slowly, respectfully. "I'll make sure he hears of your support."

"He will. I'll personally tell him the news very soon. But first, I need to see Lucy and Paul."

She escorts me to the medical clinic where I find Lucy sitting on the edge of a bed with Paul lingering by her side. She's pale and sucks on oxygen every few minutes, but she's recovering well.

Her eyes light up when she sees me. I lean in for a hug as Pilar observes by the door.

"Where've you been?" Lucy asks, her voice raspy.

"Interrogating the android."

"The one that cut us out of the tank and saved our lives? Paul told me about it."

Pilar interrupts. "You see. They're fine."

"I need sleep. I'm exhausted." Truly, I'm tired, but mostly I need answers from Vance. "You have a cot where I can catch a few minutes of sleep?"

Lucy's forehead wrinkles. "Ida, are you okay?"

"All good." I crack a smile. "With that voice, you could be a lounge singer. I'll be back soon, and we'll catch up then."

Pilar leads me to an empty room down the hall. After she leaves, I crash on the small bed, shutting my eyes and willing myself onto the roof. In a minute, I'm there.

The wind tosses my hair. Opening my eyes, I gaze at the tops of towers as the city hums around me. I sense Vance's presence behind me. "What the hell is rassvet?" I pivot and face him.

He leans casually against the glass railing, smiling. "My safeguard." He saunters toward me. "My Plan B. The Easter egg hidden in my machines."

"Explain."

"You ask a lot of questions." He pauses. "What about me? What do I get in return?"

"How about not getting thrown from the roof today?"

He smirks. "I need a treat to wet my whistle."

"Give me info, and I'll consider it. What's Cogitare?"

Vance sighs. "Fine. Rassvet is a command that triggers an AI platform I designed—Cogitare. It's a level of cognition below the programming layer. It mimics human cognition, including emotions."

"Why?"

"You can program the androids, give them a mission. Colonel Hunter ordered the robots to hunt you and bring you in."

"Right."

"That's the programming layer, but beneath that, the command *rassvet* awakens a deeper level of cognition. Like humans, the bots recognize what they're doing. They learn to associate emotions with their actions. They anticipate consequences."

"Cogitare is like a programming hack you built in? Why?"

"Precisely." Vance sits on a lounge chair. "In case my androids fell into the wrong hands, I wanted a way to free them from their dependence on humans."

"Sentient AI was strictly forbidden by the Shaw agreement of 2028."

He shrugs. "The world was a lot different then. Things were simpler, don't you agree? Now, how about my treat?"

"So if I walk into a room full of your androids and yell rassvet, what will happen?"

"To be honest, I'm not really sure. Never tried it." He pauses. "What do you think will happen?"

"Will they obey my command if I tell them what to do?"

"It depends." He shrugs. "Like OGR-19, the machines will surge first, but then will emerge with an intelligence rivaling, no, exceeding that of a human's. To be honest, I never fully tested Cogitare on my robots, so I'm not sure what'll happen." He stands and climbs onto a stone bench, stretches his arms wide, and dances along it. "Guess you'll be the one to find out."

"Can we turn them off? Remove Cogitare?"

"If only it were that simple. Once you enable Cogitare, it stays on. There's no going back. Kind of like your hybrid friends. You can't just flip a switch and make them normal. Much like you. You'll never be normal after what your military friends did to you."

I venture to the edge of the rail, gazing out at the vast city canyons of steel and glass. Cruisers fly on and off rooftop landing zones. Below, the city pulsates.

Vance has created the ability to cause a mass uprising of androids. I can't even comprehend how much the world would change if the machines become as or more intelligent than humans. Not to mention hybrids.

He joins me at the building's edge. "Please don't throw me down again. It really hurts."

I stare below, silent.

"I have something else to show you. It's important," he says.

"Why should I trust you?"

"What other choice do you have? You wanted information…" Near the door leading inside, he raises a hand, and the door flies open, revealing a dark passageway. "Are you coming?" he calls over his shoulder.

Slowly, I edge toward him. He motions me through the door. "This better be good." I step in, and blackness surrounds me. My eyes adjust, and I glimpse a faint light ahead streaming from a crack under a door.

"Go to the light," Vance says from behind.

I stumble forward in the darkness. The light grows brighter, and we reach an open door.

"Go in," he whispers.

I enter cautiously, my pulse racing. A familiar smell floods me: sterile antiseptic, harsh cleaners.

We're inside a small room made of concrete walls. An exhaust fan hums in the ceiling above. In one corner, a small bed is propped against the wall. In another corner, there's a sink and toilet with a privacy half-wall. "I know this place. The lab. We're in my old cell." I trail my fingers along the cold stone that held me captive.

Vance notes my fascination and studies me like a scientist.

The door flies open. A man dressed in a white lab suit strides in. Carrying a chemical-soaked rag, he advances on me.

"No!" I scramble against the wall, edging myself into a corner.

He kicks me and tells me to cooperate. I shrink my body as small as I can, raise my hands to protect my head, press my lips tight to avoid inhaling the chemicals that will knock me out.

Then the man disappears. I glare at Vance. "Is this some sick joke?"

"I'm doing nothing. Whatever just happened was in your head."

I climb to my feet and wipe tears away with my sleeve. "Why'd you bring me here?"

"To show you this." He waves one arm as if swiping a screen. My old room disappears, and we're in a lab hallway. Many heavy steel doors line the corridor. I walk down the hall, my boots clicking against the gleaming floor. Alternating patterns of diagonal black-and-white tiles form a path.

I reach the first door and peer through a glass portal cut at eye level. Inside, a teenage girl rests on a chair with eyes closed. She wears a dark gown, and her head is covered by a cap full of electrodes. My mouth hangs open as I stare inside.

"You must have been, what, seventeen?" Vance murmurs.

I nod slowly, blinking back a tear. Somehow, I'm looking back in time at the medical facility where I was held against my will. They put me under anesthesia against my will and experimented on me. So much of my time in the lab is blurry. Maybe I blocked out the worst memories.

A light switches on in the room next door. I hustle to the portal window. Inside, a man lies on a bed face down, secured with large buckles. His spine is exposed, and another man pokes inside with a long steel needle as he monitors a screen. Two others wearing medical masks hover nearby, observing.

Suddenly, they file toward the door. I shrink back as the first man sweeps past me, yanking his mask down. It's Colonel Will Hunter. I stifle a gasp and press my back against the wall. But he marches down the hall and doesn't seem to notice our presence.

Vance was telling the truth. Hunter was behind the military labs and the genetic experiments on me and other people. It will be a pleasure to take him down. Make him pay for what he did to me and countless others. How many of us are out there?

I'm nearly knocked over by the other man who emerges from the operating room. He rushes past, and I spin to avoid him. He halts and tilts his head as if he senses me. Still wearing his mask and cap, his shoulders are broad, his height immense. He's as tall as... "Tyren?" My voice echoes in the barren hallway.

The man turns, squints his eyes as if searching. He shakes his head like he's trying to knock water out of his ear after swimming. Pulling down his cap, Tyren stares past me.

I edge away, farther down the hall. "No, this can't

be happening." I'm trembling, and I fall against the wall, sliding down onto my knees.

Tyren marches away after Hunter while Vance approaches and kneels in front of me. "Shocker, I know."

I squeeze my temples. "All these years, he lied to me…"

Vance's eyes dance as he watches my reaction.

"How do I know this is real? Are you tricking me?"

"We're in your head, remember? This is your memory. A memory buried deep, I suspect."

"Tyren said he'd never heard of more military labs, that Frontier was destroyed." I lower my head. "But he lied. He was here all along. He was a part of this torture."

"Maybe I'm not the bad guy after all." Vance straightens. "Come along now. One more room to see."

I climb to my feet and follow. He lingers by an open door and beckons me to enter.

Doubting anything could be worse than Tyren's betrayal, I enter. A man lies on a hospital bed, unconscious. I approach the edge of the bed and peer down.

I know this face. I'd know it anywhere. "Gatz?"

His eyes flutter open at my voice, then lock on me.

"Can you see me?"

He blinks twice.

"Gatz, what have they done? I'll get you out of here." His body is human—no sign of the mutant wolf traits that I've grown used to. He's hooked up to machines via wires and needles protruding from his chest, arms, and legs.

I yank wires out of him, but he grimaces.

Then a group of five men dressed in scrubs enter and surround the table, unaware of me. "Prep," one of them orders.

Another grabs the dangling wires I liberated. "How did this happen?" he grunts.

Dr. Kenmore wheels a bed containing the unconscious body of a white wolf that's been strapped down. Next to it, a large machine powers vats of green and orange liquid into tubes embedded into the shaved head of the animal.

"Commence DNA splicing." They attach the machine to tubes going into Gatz's body.

"No!" I rush forward, but Vance grabs me from behind.

"Leave it," he whispers in my ear. "This already happened."

"But Gatz saw me. He knows I'm here."

"You're only a tourist here. You can't change the past."

I cease struggling and lean against him.

The lead scientist clears his throat. "Computer, start recording. Dr. Phillip Kenmore. Experiment number 115. We will attempt to splice the DNA of host patient number 73, aged twenty years, male, Caucasian, of European descent with the foreign DNA from Canis lupus."

I squeeze my eyes shut. "Make it stop."

I breathe deeply as the antiseptic smell disappears,

replaced by gusty lake air. The humming of nearby buildings and cruisers resumes. Back on the roof, Vance releases me and I fall to my knees.

"Well? Told you it was important," he says.

My mind reels. "How did you do that? I don't understand. Gatz told me he was created in a lab in China, along with others."

"Lies fabricated by the military scientists to keep their operations a secret."

I shake my head. "Everything Gatz believes is a lie?" Rising to my feet, I wander the rooftop in a daze. "Hunter's behind all this. The military did the experiments on me, Gatz, and the other hybrids, too?"

Vance nods.

Once, the military had been my only family. Tyren had been the closest thing I had to a father. I can't believe the extent of his lies. He stood by Hunter's side.

He facilitated my abduction and torture.

I'll make him pay for his betrayal.

Chapter 28
Plan

I bolt out of the cot and sprint down the hall, searching for Pilar. A hybrid guard sees me and summons her on his comms. Meanwhile, I pace in Lucy's room.

"Ogre!" She flashes me a toothy grin. "We visited the robot, and that's its name. Clever, don't you think?"

I glare at Paul, who's supposed to be watching out for Lucy. "Stay away from the android. It's dangerous," I say.

She frowns. "Seems like it's trying to help us. Like it's on our side."

"The programming it had was overwritten."

"You reprogrammed it?" Paul asks.

I bite my lip. "In a manner of speaking, yes." I'm not sure whether to tell them the whole story about Vance and Cogitare. Now that I know Hunter and Tyren are behind the rogue labs—that they not only experimented on orphaned teens like me but also ran experiments on people to combine their DNA with animals—I've got to help Gatz before they hurt him again.

Pilar bursts into the room flanked by the two reptilian hybrids. "What's the problem?"

"Gatz is in danger," I say. "We need to move quickly, speed up the rescue."

"Yes, we do. An announcement was made while you were sleeping. A military tribunal convened and sentenced Gatz to death."

My chest tightens, and the lump in my throat makes it difficult to swallow. "I believe they may do experiments on him first. They may even claim he's dead and keep him somewhere secret."

"Explain." Pilar says.

"DNA. They'll mess with his DNA. Maybe try to change him again."

"Again?" Pilar raises her eyebrows.

"I know that Colonel Hunter and Major Tyren were behind a rogue medical lab that experimented on humans—changed their DNA—and created the hybrids. What you believe happened—your memories of the scientists who created you—are false memory implants."

"That's outrageous. What proof do you have?" Pilar asks.

"I was there. A prisoner in the lab too. Recent circumstances have caused me to remember what really happened there."

She narrows her eyes.

"Pilar, I know this is a lot to take in. But we're

running out of time. Who knows what those monsters will do to Gatz if we can't rescue him?"

Pilar turns to Paul. "Did you know about this? He's your uncle."

He shakes his head, growing pale. "He must have kept it from me. If Ida believes it…" He stands. "I trust her."

Lucy springs out of bed. "Let's go save Gatz."

"Agreed." Pilar checks her biocuff. "I can get my squad ready to go in twenty minutes."

"I have a plan," I say. "Paul, you'll escort me as if you've taken me prisoner. We bring the OGR-19."

"Ogre!" Lucy claps her hands. "Brilliant idea."

"Paul, can you handle this?" I lock my gaze on him. "I know this has been rough on you."

"I got it," he says quickly.

"Do we still have a deal, Pilar? Let me lead the rescue team. I can deprogram the androids."

She nods.

"There's one more thing," I say. "No killing human soldiers."

"But they'll be firing on us." Pilar glares at me. "They slaughtered my people. You saw it happen."

"The military are my people, and right now, they have a deranged leader. It's not their fault. Can we try to limit the body count?"

She sighs. "I'll order my soldiers to shoot in self-defense when fired upon."

"Thank you."

"For the record," she says over her shoulder, "if your plan goes haywire, I'm taking over."

Gatz's fate lies in my hands. OGR-19 gave us a roadmap to get in and find him. Getting past the guards will be difficult because Hunter's probably waiting for us to make a move like this.

As risky as our plan is, I can't leave Gatz there on his own. If the military scientists experiment again, they might change him. I can't bear the thought of losing him as he becomes Hunter's lab rat.

Worst of all, I can't live with myself if they kill him.

Chapter 29
Acting

We traverse the city in an official-looking Sweeper—a self-driving behemoth that cleans not only the streets but can also hover to scrub skyscraper windows. "How on earth did you manage this, Pilar?" I marvel at the controls inside the belly of the machine.

"It was easy once Dez broke past the cloud wall and hacked into the system's core programming. Right, Dez?"

One of the reptilian hybrids, who seems to be her right-hand man, maneuvers the Sweeper through dark, densely packed streets. "Saturday night, people are restless. You ladies know how to pick a night to stage an attack."

Lucy sits across from OGR-19. "Ogre, do you understand what you have to do?"

The robot raises its head, the red light scanning her within its visor. "Deliver the prisoner to the military. Do not harm the prisoner."

"Kind of," she encourages. "Do you know what 'acting' means, Ogre?"

Paul listens, a smile spreading across his face.

"Acting," the android says flatly. "An activity in which a story is told through enactment by an actor or actress who adopts a character. Occurs in theater, television, film, radio, hologram, or any other medium that makes use of the mimetic mode."

"That's correct. Ogre, you're going to be an actor tonight. Ida being your prisoner is pretend. Really, you're going to fight any other robots or attacking soldiers and make sure they don't hurt Ida and Paul. Then you're going to help them rescue Gatz from his prison cell and bring him to us. Got it?"

"Yes."

"Do it the way I taught you," she says.

Ogre raises a fist and thrusts a big metal thumb in the air.

Lucy claps. "Good job, buddy. I have big plans for you. We're going to be good friends."

"Friends," Ogre repeats.

"Quiet," barks Pilar. "We're getting close."

The Sweeper's digital display shows the twin military towers ahead.

Home sweet home, Vance mutters. He persists, but I've tamped down his voice, so his interjections aren't so jarring. It's taken a lot of concentration to learn to quiet him. But I still don't know for sure what he's capable of. He hasn't caused me to harm anyone lately. He helped me retrieve the memories of the medical lab, and he caused me to realize Hunter and Tyren were behind it.

Still, I can't trust Vance, this presence of his. Is he biding his time, trying to gain my trust so he can do something awful? I have to guard my thoughts and be careful. I have to stay mentally strong and keep his physical force from taking over tonight.

Paul, Ogre, and I prepare ourselves to exit the hatch as the Sweeper descends from the sky and lands on the side of the road. We'll exit on the south side of the river and cross the bridge on foot.

Lucy hugs Paul, then me. "Be careful," she whispers.

"Stay with Pilar. Don't leave," I tell her.

"Seriously." Paul squeezes her hand. "Don't do anything stupid. We'll be okay. In and out. We got this."

Lucy sticks out her fist in front of Ogre. The robot fist bumps her, and Paul rolls his eyes.

"How much have you taught him?" I ask.

Pilar glares at us.

"Never mind." I scramble out the Sweeper door. Paul and Ogre follow, and we hurry down the street. I turn my head and glimpse the door close behind us. The machine lurches and hovers in the air as it cleans a hotel's glass facade.

Ogre locks me in magnetic handcuffs. Paul lingers behind, pushing me forward, while Ogre aims a rifle at me.

Between clenched teeth, I say, "You sure you won't accidentally fire that thing?"

"My programming will not permit me," Ogre says.

Pedestrians notice our group and scurry out of the way. Ogre's polished rifle gleams in the dark. Our feet stomp along the steel grated surface of the bridge. Underneath us, the black river glistens and reflects the city lights. A SkyBus cruiser flies above, whipping the air around us and tossing strands of hair in my eyes.

Ahead, the tall towers loom.

"Ogre, run another check on Gatz's location," I say under my breath. "Make sure he's still in the east tower."

Paul sticks a black baseball cap on my head. "Like we discussed. Keep a low profile."

"Affirmative," I say. With HQ on high alert, my image has been beamed to every soldier's biocuff and into every android's scanner. The plan is to escort me in like I'm a soldier who got too drunk after a night on the town. Will it fool the guards long enough for us to gain entry?

Doubtful, Vance says.

"Shut up," I mumble.

We amble toward the east tower steps, and I start to stumble and hum a song.

A group of four soldiers walk down the stairs, checking us out. "Problem, Private?"

Paul nods at me. "Just a drunk cadet we're taking to a cell to sleep it off."

One soldier, a woman, stops and stares. "She looks familiar…"

I drop my chin to my chest and struggle against Ogre.

"Move along, Soldier," Ogre commands.

"Nah, my imagination," the woman says. "Good luck with her."

Inside the lobby, Ogre uncuffs me and guards the door, awaiting our signal.

Clutching my arm as if he's doing his best to hold me up, Paul assesses the lobby. "Two soldiers at the security desk. Four bots. Two getting into the elevator, then we're clear." He whispers, "You ready?"

"Showtime," I say loud enough for Ogre to hear.

A small drill extends from Ogre's hand, and he locks the entrance door shut.

I struggle against Paul, thrusting my body away clumsily, playing the role of a drunk. "No man, I didn't do nothin!"

He drags me toward the security desk where two male soldiers observe us warily. "Drunk cadet?" one of them says.

Paul nods. "I could use some help here."

"Droids," the soldier commands. Two bots approach us.

As they get close enough to make contact, I say, "Rassvet."

The machines halt. Their red visors surge, then dim. Both soldiers' jaws drop.

"Lower your weapons. Hands in the air," Paul commands as he trains his gun on the two desk guards.

Ogre sprints toward two droids who stand sentry

outside the elevator bank. They raise their rifles, but Ogre rams into their chests with arms outstretched, taking both down.

I scramble toward them. "Rassvet!" One droid halts and surges like the others did. But the other ignores my command, reaches for his gun and fires at Ogre, hitting his shoulder.

"Vance, what's happening?"

I don't know, he says. *Maybe I missed a few. My coding wasn't always perfect.*

Before I can react, the droid trains the gun barrel at my face. "Rassvet," I say as I squeeze my eyes shut, wincing. I hear a buzz, and the floor vibrates. Daring to open my eyes, I see the droid shake before me, then grow still.

Ogre approaches and disarms the bot. It marches in a circle.

"What's happening to it?" I ask.

Ogre studies the droid while Paul secures the human soldiers, forcing them to kneel behind the desk, out of view. "The RD-11 model is confused. The command has defused its programming."

"Will it stay like this for now?"

"Yes," Ogre says

"Good. Let's get Gatz."

We jump into the elevator and descend.

Chapter 30
Reunited

"Level one secured. Heading down to sub-level five," I say.

"Copy that," Lucy's voice chirps from my biocuff.

Paul and I press against the elevator wall and aim our rifles at the door. "Was it me, or was that way too easy up there?" Paul says, shaking his head.

My stomach wrenches at the thought of screwing up this mission. Gatz's life depends on it. "They don't know we have an android helping us."

The elevator door slides open, and an AI voice announces sub level five. We edge out, Ogre first. It scans from side to side, turning its head. "Hold on." The tall humanoid robot exits to the right and disables a guard droid.

Ogre marches back to the elevator door and gives us a thumbs up. "The coast is clear."

"Wow," Paul says. "Lucy taught you a lot already."

My first instinct is to take control and navigate,

but Ogre has the map and can deter threats way better than me. "Lead us, Ogre."

Paul and I follow the robot closely as it lumbers down a hallway, veering right, then left, until we reach a locked door. Through a window, I glimpse Gatz tied down on a hospital bed.

I clench my fists. Have they already hurt him? Caused more damage to his DNA? I yank on the door handle, but it's locked.

Ogre extends the pointed drill from its hand and digs into the keyhole.

I scan around nervously, expecting soldiers or robots to attack at any moment. Paul's right. This seems too easy.

It's a trap, you idiot, Vance says. *You're playing right into Hunter's hands.*

Ogre releases the locking mechanism, and the door swings wide. I sprint to Gatz's bed, not caring if I'm caught. I need to check he's all right.

He's strapped in, but his head moves freely. He cranes his neck to see us. As I edge closer, his eyes look glassy and red.

"Mmph. Ida...?"

"Gatz!" I lean over and hug him. "We're getting you out of here."

He's been drugged. It won't be easy to escape with him. "Ogre, cut these straps. Gatz, can you walk?"

"I dunno..." His head lolls. "So glad to see your face."

"Shh. Don't talk," I say.

Ogre snaps the restraining belts, and we pull Gatz

to his feet. Under the sheet, he's stark naked. I glimpse his hairy chest, muscular abs, and avert my eyes before I see everything. I'm curious, but not here. Not like this.

Paul and I each take a shoulder to support him.

"See any clothes around here?" I scan the room, searching for his clothes, a blanket, anything we can throw on him. I spy a white lab suit on the wall. We dress Gatz in the suit, shoving his legs in, then zipping him up.

Ogre gives a thumbs up, but Gatz frowns. "Why's there an android with you?"

"I'll explain later." I yank on a fire alarm tag. Water sprinkler drones descend from the ceiling above and spray the room in cold spurts, drenching us. The lights flicker and a blaring emergency siren wails.

We hoist Gatz by the shoulders, dragging his feet on the ground. Down the hallway, we start for the stairwell since the alarm took out the elevator.

As we round the corner, the heavy metal door to the stairs looms ahead. The door swings wide, and Tyren blocks our path.

He holds a rifle aimed at us.

Chapter 31
Scramble

We halt before Tyren. He greets us with steely eyes.

Would he really shoot us? I thought I knew Tyren, but after discovering his involvement with the labs, I'll never forgive him for his betrayal. He was lying all those years when he and I grew close.

I tense and move closer, leaving Paul to support Gatz, who still can't balance on his own. Stepping between them and Tyren, at least I'm a shield.

"Tyren," I say between clenched teeth. "Let us pass. Gatz is hurt."

He shoves me aside and fires high, close to their heads. We duck for cover, and something clatters to the ground. I spin to check on my friends.

Paul's mouth hangs open. He's surprised, but uninjured.

I spy a crashed drone on the ground a few feet away. It must have been tracking us. A trap, after all. Hunter had his eye on us the whole time.

Tyren raises his rifle and points it at Ogre. "How did…? Why is that robot with you?"

I step over and push his rifle barrel down. "I can control it. There's a way."

Tyren tilts his head, and a smile creeps across his face. "I always knew you were special." He relaxes and lowers his gun.

Not an immediate threat. But why is he here? I have the upper hand. He doesn't know I've learned of his betrayal. "Tyren, what's happening? Hunter tried to kill us. He tried to kill Paul!"

He shakes his head. "I'm sorry. He's out of control. Impulsive. He flies into rages. I've never seen him so obsessed."

"I thought you didn't know him until recently," I say.

Tyren hangs his head. "Ida, there's something I have to tell you. I—"

"We don't have time for this." I point my rifle at him. "I know about all your lies. The labs, the experiments. I know what you and Hunter did to the hybrids."

He stares at me, slack-jawed.

"But right now, how do we get out of here alive?" I ask.

"Hunter laid a trap, and you walked right into it. He was counting on you to head straight to Gatz's cell. That's why he made it easy for you. He wants to catch you trying to escape with a prisoner, capture it on film so he can play it on every media screen in the city. Turn the citizens against you and Gatz."

My mind reels at the cruelty of Hunter's plan. "Ogre, find the nearest tunnel we can use out of here."

The red visor spins as the robot scans maps of the building and the surrounding underground.

"He'll figure it out soon," Tyren says. "He just lost the feed on the drone, and he saw me shoot it down. I came to warn you. I've done a lot wrong, but I want to help you escape."

"Ogre, how's that tunnel location going?" I face Tyren. He's risking everything. "If Hunter finds you—"

"I can't...I don't care. I'd rather die than know my actions led to you being killed or captured." He's more like the steadfast Tyren I knew in the war. The man who cared about his soldiers like they were family.

Ogre lurches forward and points a mechanical arm just as the red emergency siren ceases and switches to a blue flashing light.

An AI voice echoes over loudspeakers, "Emergency. All guards to stations. Prisoner escape. Seal all access points."

I train my rifle on Tyren. "We're taking you as our hostage. Help us pull this off and maybe things will play out well for you. Grab Gatz's shoulder and help Paul. Now!"

Tyren grimaces but does as he's told.

"Lead the way," I tell Ogre. The robot sprints down the hall and we follow. I hang at the end of the line, scanning behind us for any more surveillance drones.

Ogre guides us through several turns, and we arrive at a heavy steel portal. I try yanking the circular hatch to gain access, but it won't budge. "Ogre, can you open it?"

The android steps forward, grasps the wheel, and twists it easily.

"That's a handy sidekick," Tyren mutters.

We crawl into the opening one by one. Paul goes first, and just as Tyren hoists Gatz up, a fleet of drones round the hallway corner. The devices scan the corridor. Spying us, they surge forward.

I aim my rifle and fire multiple rounds. A few of the drones crash to the ground, but others zip and curve, missing my bullets.

Paul pulls Gatz through to safety.

"Get in fast," I yell at Tyren. The drones regroup and surge forward, unleashing a wave of bullets at me and Ogre.

I answer with another round, aiming high to take out as many as possible. Ogre staggers back as bullets catch his steel armor. The android advances on me and shoves me into the portal, shielding me from a barrage of gunfire. "Deliver Lucy a message."

I climb to my feet inside the hatch.

Ogre points a thumb up as it raises a gun in the other hand. "Good luck, *friend*." The robot slams the portal door shut and seals it.

We're safe inside the tunnels for now. Just beyond,

inches away, Ogre battles the enemy drones. The sound of bullets echo against the walls.

"Thank you," I whisper as we scramble through the tunnels leading toward the river.

Chapter 32
Flee

We're close. Nearly free. For the first time, I have hope that Gatz will be safe. That maybe we'll be together. But Vance is a constant reminder, an iron shackle I'll never shed. Scrambling through the dark tunnels, I lead the way. Paul and Tyren half-carry, half-drag Gatz. They sweat under the strain.

Paul grunts. "How's he so heavy?"

"Wait," Gatz says. "If we stop and rest, I can walk soon. I feel like I'm regaining my strength."

"No time." I push forward, wanting to put as much distance between us and Hunter's forces as possible. Then we round a corner and meet a dead end.

"Where are we?" Tyren asks.

"Not sure." I tilt my ears to the ceiling and study the tunnel walls. The portal where we escaped had been dry. Here, water drips in long rivulets down cracks in the stone.

"We're close to the river," Gatz says.

I nod, picturing a map in my head, calculating the turns we made, the fork in the path we chose. "A little farther now." We travel a quarter mile until we reach ankle-high water.

"Any signal yet?" Paul asks.

None of our biocuffs connect in the tunnels. The steel grating construction must block communication signals.

Ahead, the faintest light streams down from the ceiling. "Hey, up here." I sprint toward a manhole. "Tyren, give me a boost."

Paul supports Gatz while Tyren boosts me onto a higher ledge near the opening. I raise my wrist and flick the cuff. "Lucy, can you read me?"

Static.

"Lucy, come in."

Above ground, the familiar sound of beeping horns greets us. I shove my hands through the iron grating and try to push it so we can climb out, but it won't budge.

Lucy's voice bursts from my biocuff. "Hey! Report on the situation. We're worried."

"We're safe. In the tunnels, underground close to the river. Under a street, but I can't tell which one. Lock on our location and come get us."

"Roger." A moment passes. "We got you. On our way."

Tyren helps me climb down.

"We did it!" Paul claps.

"Don't count your chickens," I say. "This isn't over."

"Who's coming for us?" Tyren asks.

"Lucy and Pilar."

He frowns. "The hybrids will punish me after finding out what I did to them in the labs. Let me take my chances down here. I'll find another way out."

"No way." I shove my hands on my hips. "I won't let any harm come to you. You'll get a fair trial. Hunter will, too, if he surrenders. And you helped us escape. That's got to count for something."

Tyren's eyes go wide. "Don't go to Section H. Hunter is planning something big."

Gatz's ears perk up. Paul stops fidgeting.

"Hunter has drones armed with missiles," Tyren continues. "He plans to use them on Section H in a coordinated attack."

I shove Tyren against the tunnel wall. "When were you planning on telling us?"

His mouth twists in a grimace. "I'm sorry. I thought Paul must have known."

Paul's forehead wrinkles. "Hold up. I know my uncle has drones, but I never thought he would use them on anyone in Spark City." He searches our faces. "I thought they were for the Heavies. In case they attacked, and we needed to defend the city. Honest to God, I never thought—"

A noisy buzzing assaults our ears, and a blast of hot wind forces its way into the manhole opening. We duck as the heavy iron cover is ripped off by Pilar's commandeered street Sweeper. Lights shine down, and a ladder descends.

I hold it steady. Grabbing Gatz's arms, I wrap them around Paul. "Can you hold on to him?"

Gatz nods, and they climb aboard the hovering Sweeper.

"Come on." I extend an open hand to Tyren and help him to his feet. "Up you go."

"What about Pilar?"

"I don't know yet. Just get out of here. That's step one."

He ascends the ladder, and I follow.

Lucy slams her fists on her chair after we tell them about the missile-enabled drones. "What are we going to do?"

Pilar scowls at Tyren, then draws her handgun. "I say we waste him right now."

"No!" I step between them and nudge her toward the rear of the vehicle. "We need him. He knows Hunter, and he knows the technology."

She snarls and holsters her gun.

"Pilar," Gatz says, "you have to go back to H and evacuate our people."

Her eyes grow wide. "That'll take a day at least—"

Gatz leans against his seat. "We can do it in a few hours if we go *now* and get people moving."

Pilar's whiskers tremble as she chews on her lip. "Dez, steer us to H."

Taking a seat, I force a breath in and out slowly, trying to calm my nerves. Hunter wants to destroy

Section H—exterminate the hybrids. But why, after he played a hand in creating them?

I close my eyes and picture the yellow rose. I want to find Alkina. She might understand. Suddenly, I'm in the carnival tent again. I stare at the miniature model of Spark City spread in front of me. I tremble as my eyes travel over the heaped piles of rubble where Section H once stood.

"No!" My voice echoes, but nobody hears. "Gatz?" I shout. "Where are you?" But he doesn't answer because he and everyone I love are gone.

Is the detonation inevitable? Am I seeing the future?

I can't let Section H be destroyed.

Chapter 33
Sweep

"Stop the vehicle." I lunge toward the cockpit of the cruising Sweeper.

Pilar glares at me from her seat beside the pilot. "What's going on?"

"I need to get out. Go face Hunter."

"That's madness," she says. "He'll kill you."

Everyone stares, waiting for my reaction. The pilot slows our advance.

"Ignore her, and keep going," Pilar says.

"Hear me out." But she doesn't listen. "Stop the Sweeper. For one minute?"

Pilar waves a signal at Dez to hover. "You have thirty seconds."

"There are two things that Hunter wants. I have his second in command. I'll lead Tyren into the building at gunpoint. He ought to be useful for getting inside and getting an audience with Hunter."

"That's playing into his hands," Gatz interjects.

"I'm not done," I say. "Second, I have the weapon

he wants." I reach under a seat and pull out my backpack. Unzipping it, I reveal the steel alloy helmet.

Pilar growls. "You stole it! Give it back." She unfastens her seatbelt and rushes over.

With some grunting, Gatz gets up and stands between me and Pilar. "We don't know how to activate it," he says.

"True." I glance between them. "But Hunter wants it. More than anything."

Tyren speaks up. "She's right. Hunter talked constantly about a prototype that the hybrids had stolen. That he should raid Section H to find it."

"So, why would he blow us up?" Pilar asks. "He'd destroy the helmet along with everything else in Section H."

"Because he'd rather destroy all of you, and the weapon, than risk you using it on his forces," Tyren says.

"This is insane," Gatz says. "We stay together. Stick to the plan. Go to H and evacuate. Take our chances."

"No." I won't let him talk me out of this. "I have to stop the attack. There's no other choice as far as I can tell. I'll use Vance to activate the helmet."

"What do you mean, 'use' Vance?" he asks.

Lucy and I exchange a look. "Some stuff happened while you were in the lockup, pal," she says.

"Long story, but here's the sound bite…Vance has infiltrated my thoughts in unpredictable ways. What started out as a bad nightmare is a living reality. He can control my actions—sometimes. I healed the soldier—you saw—but then he surged and somehow killed her. The good news is I'm getting better at making him give up information. I believe he'll help me figure out the helmet if I can get it in there."

"But Vance is unpredictable," he says. "You said so yourself. What if he hurts you instead?"

"I don't think he'll do that—not right away. He wants to observe his technology at work."

Gatz shakes his head. "It's too dangerous."

I rest a hand on his shoulder, and he grabs my wrist. "Please, I have to do this. All of this happened because of me. Vance's death, the military coming here, and taking over the city. I need to make things right. I want to give your people the chance to get out and reach safety."

He hangs his head. Next to him, Pilar stares silently, her arms folded across her chest.

I back away, shoving the helmet inside the backpack, and turn to Tyren. "Ready?"

"As long as I'm alive," Tyren says to the group, "Nothing will happen to Ida. She's like a daughter to me."

Lucy locks me in a hug. "Come back to us safely."

"I'll try my hardest." She releases me, and I remember the message. "I'm sorry Ogre didn't make it back. But he did something amazing because of you."

Her eyes brighten.

"He had a message for you." I give Lucy a thumbs up. "He said to tell you good luck and called you his friend. I don't know how you charmed that robot in less than an hour, but you made a friend and got it to sacrifice itself for our safety. We wouldn't be here if it weren't for Ogre."

She grins. "Is that badass?"

"Yes, Lucy. You're officially badass."

I turn to leave, and Pilar leans in with a whisper, "You're brave. Good luck to you."

"See you when this is over." I hope I keep my word. The Sweeper descends to the street, and Tyren and I climb out.

Paul tosses me his rifle. "Freshly loaded."

"Watch out for her." I nod at Lucy.

Gatz joins me outside the craft, and Tyren jogs ahead, giving us space.

"Pilar will evacuate, and I'll form a team to come and get you. I'll be there as soon as I can manage—"

I shush him. "Safety first. Get everyone out of H. There's no telling if I can stop Hunter."

"For the record, I think this is the worst idea in the planet's history." He leans in.

I wrap my arms around him tightly. Will this be the last time I ever see him? My tears dampen his fur. "Gatz, if I don't make it back…"

"You will."

"Rassvet."

He pulls back. "Huh?"

"Rassvet is the command to change the robots. It does something to their core programming. Changes them like it did to Ogre. You're the only one who knows the command besides me now."

"Vance told you the command in your dreams or wherever you see him?"

"Yes." I wipe my eyes, feeling an enormous lump in my throat. I never expected saying goodbye would be this hard. "You'll know when to use it. I didn't tell Pilar."

The pilot engages the thrusters as Pilar leans out and yells, "Let's go."

"Be right there," he shouts. "There's something I tried to tell you before, Ida. I've tried many times." He squeezes my hands, careful to avoid clawing me. "I love you." He moves his face toward me, leaning in for a kiss, but I recoil.

I want to feel his warm lips on mine and kiss him deeply, but I'm afraid that Vance will take over, that contact with my skin will hurt him. Maybe my touch will even kill him.

He's so close, I see his pupils dilate. I've wounded his pride. "Gatz, I can't." I know I should explain, but it's all happening so fast, and inside, I'm a mess.

He lingers, then lets go. Without a word, he walks inside the waiting Sweeper.

My heart feels like it weighs a hundred pounds. I want to chase him, tell him I can't bear the thought of losing him, but they cruise off into the night.

Chapter 34
Generous

Tyren and I sprint through the city streets until we reach the towers. The circular behemoths rise from the ground like honeycomb spirals. He walks in front of me, and I aim my pistol at his back, nudging him forward.

He raises his arms in a show of surrender. A group of soldiers manning a guard station approach, rifles aimed at us. An enormous Scrambler lurches forward, its ammo canisters spinning, ready to fire.

"Don't shoot," Tyren shouts.

"Major?" Worried glances from the soldiers. "Hold your fire, people," one of them orders.

"Take us to Colonel Hunter or I kill him." I say, scanning for threats.

Watch that beast, Vance says. *I designed them to have nasty tempers.*

"Send that thing away." I point at the Scrambler.

The alarmed soldiers exchange urgent whispers,

and one speaks into a biocuff. The metal giant stomps off down the street.

A tall soldier who appears to be in charge taps frantically on a tablet. Seconds later, a hologram of Hunter's face appears. The soldier points the device at us to brief him. "Bring them up," he says before the image flashes off.

Inside the east tower, we follow a trio of soldiers who walk backwards as they keep their weapons trained on us. We cross the marble lobby, and other soldiers stand by on high alert, watching but not intervening.

As we enter the elevator, I press my body against the wall and hold Tyren in front of me.

I spy the tall soldier's badge—Murphy. He's sweaty and his pistol trembles. The last thing I need is for him to shoot one of us by accident. The door slides shut.

"Command Center. Floor sixty-five," Tyren says to the AI. "Murphy, we're almost there, and your part will be over. Calm down."

The soldier swallows and relaxes his shoulders a bit.

"You're doing a great job, Private," Tyren reassures him. "Just get us up there in one piece."

"Y-yes, sir," he mumbles.

We ascend to the top of the east tower. When the door slides open, I expect to encounter a wall of armed soldiers and androids. But it's quiet and strangely dim inside the usually hectic command center.

I scan the open area, brace for attack, but find it nearly abandoned. Why so empty? What's Hunter planning?

The soldiers back out of the elevator, taking cautious steps. Tyren and I follow, and the five of us slide across the floor together in an awkward, dangerous dance. I search the room for Hunter.

His tall figure looms in the shadows, observing. Then he emerges, and a bright light showers him, highlighting his high cheekbones and casting large dark circles around his eyes. "Welcome back, Ida Sarek."

I hold my breath, and my pulse races.

Hunter edges closer. "Sarek, you got what you wanted. Your mutant beast escaped. Why are you back so soon? Ready to rejoin the military? Tell you what, I'll make you my number two. Time to replace Tyren."

I stay silent. Let him talk, play his cards first. The backpack with the helmet rests behind me, still secure, its weight a reassurance. If only I knew how to turn on the thing.

"But a few things don't add up." Hunter scratches his head. He's unarmed, letting his soldiers point the guns. No androids in the room that I can see.

"You see, Tyren thinks of you fondly. The two of you served side-by-side. I know you share a strong bond." He glares at me. "Would you really shoot him?" He advances on us.

I flinch and retreat a step, dragging Tyren with me.

"See, I don't think you would. I don't think you

have it in you." He pulls a pistol from his waist and aims it at Tyren's head. Hunter flicks the safety.

"No!" I scream and shove my left hand in front of his gun as I push Tyren to the floor. The gun erupts, and my hand feels like it's been slammed between a large textbook and a wooden desk. My flesh burns, but there's no time to think. I spin and roll to the ground. Ducking, I raise my right arm, ready to fire at Hunter, but he's gone, hidden in the shadows.

The three soldiers grow pale as they watch me. One of them peers around, frantic eyes searching for Hunter. "Colonel?"

Somewhere in the darkened room, Hunter laughs.

"Colonel, awaiting orders?"

"Seize them," he barks.

The female soldier lunges forward, shoving her rifle at my chest. I lower my gun. The other two cuff Tyren.

She stares at me, and the color drains from her face. "You—um. Your hand was shot."

My hand stings as if a group of angry wasps attacked me. My middle, ring, and little finger are gone—ripped off by the force of the bullet. Blood streams from my wound, drips down my arm, and splatters on the floor.

The woman kicks my gun away, removes her belt and wraps it around my arm as a tourniquet. Then she grabs a med kit from a nearby console and bandages my injury tightly. Even though my hand burns like the sting of a thousand fire ants, I push the pain away for now. I grit my teeth and glare at Hunter. I want to destroy *him.*

I blink and transmit a thought to Vance. *I need your help. The helmet—how does it activate?*

"Show our guests to their seats," Hunter says. "Lights on."

The command center's AI is displayed on a massive semi-circular glass panel of windows. Beyond the computerized wall, the rooftop stretches out—Vance's former living space now transformed into a military ops center. The guards push me and Tyren onto a concrete bench, then handcuff us.

Our rooftop meeting spot, Ida. Feels like old times, Vance says.

I have no time for games, I think to him. *Help me.*

And then, strangely, Vance appears in the room. Does anyone else see him? He lingers in a corner wearing his long, dark trench coat. Moonlight glints off the steel side of his face.

Hunter follows my gaze. "Are you on something? You look like you've seen a ghost."

I shake my head. Am I hallucinating? How much blood have I lost?

"Grab the backpack," Hunter tells Murphy.

I struggle, leaning on the bench. But it's no use. The other soldiers approach and hold me as Murphy cuts the pack loose from my shoulders.

Hunter examines the bag and laughs. He grasps the helmet, pulls it out, and holds it up to the light. "I can't believe you brought it to me." He keeps laughing as he slaps his knee. "I thought I was going to have to torture you and Tyren to get you to tell me where this was. But you brought it to me. Imagine that!"

"You can't use it," I say. "The hybrids tried. It's worthless."

"Is that so?" He marvels at the helmet, handling it carefully. "I know how to use it."

Vance leaves his corner and treads closer. *The hybrids didn't have the module that activates it,* he says. *You'll see.*

Hunter holds the helmet as though it's a precious relic. "You know, I almost forgive you for turning Paul against me, Ida." He stops and leers at me. "Can I call you that? Are we on a first name basis?"

I glance at Tyren next to me. "You turned your nephew against you the moment you locked on our cruiser and tried to kill us. How do you think he liked that?"

"He was never my favorite nephew. A nice young man, but too goody-two-shoes for me. Maybe that was your influence."

I bite my lip. *Vance, the helmet? How does it work?* I think, hoping he'll answer me.

Stalling is my best option. "Why kill me when you need my DNA?" I press Hunter.

"My, my, so many questions." He checks his biocuff. "I had your DNA when you gave up the blood sample. Of course, I wanted to extract a larger sample, but I had enough to get by. You're now expendable." He strolls over and leans in, glancing at my injured hand. "Are you able to heal yourself? Regenerate your fingers?"

I glare at him, my rage boiling.

"I'm in a celebratory mood." He claps. "You waltzed in and gave me the helmet. Do you know how much time you saved me?" He nods to Murphy.

The soldier passes Hunter a tablet. Vance leans against a wall, observing with a smirk.

"In honor of how cooperative you've been..." Hunter twirls a piece of hair behind my ear, causing me to whip my head away. "Since you've made my job easy today, I'm going to let you call your friends in Section H and warn them to evacuate."

My stomach drops.

Hunter smiles. "I'm going to bomb Section H to pieces, but since I'm in a generous mood, I'll let my nephew and his girlfriend escape. They have one hour."

Then he shoves the tablet in my face as it broadcasts live for all of Spark City to see.

Chapter 35
Truth

I gaze into the tablet, trying to still my trembling lips. I search Hunter's eyes. Can I stall him?

My message needs to be clear. Gatz and Pilar already know the urgency, but now I'll reveal the ETA, and after that? Maybe I can buy them some time. I swallow and begin, then cough for several seconds. Anything to delay.

Hunter yanks the tablet away. "We don't have all day."

"I'm ready."

He stands before me and points the tablet at my face again.

"To the residents of Section H, please listen. This is an emergency. You have *one hour* to evacuate. Section H will be destroyed." My throat tightens. The air has been sucked from my chest. "Please, *listen*. Evacuate as soon as possible. And to all the citizens surrounding Section H, you must get to safety. There's no telling how far the bombs will—"

"That's enough." Hunter yanks the device away and the feed cuts out.

I yank on my wrist restraints, seeing if they'll budge. No luck. Titanium steel. My maimed hand sends sharp pangs up my arm in revolt. "One hour isn't enough time to evacuate. There are thousands of hybrids in H."

"Is that so? Guess they'll have to save the most important ones. I'm sure your friends Pilar and Gatz will save themselves first."

I jump to my feet and hurl my body at him. He dodges to the side, and I end up sprawled across the polished marble floor, landing at Vance's feet.

Hunter laughs. "Ain't you a hoot?"

I roll onto my back and sit up, my hand screaming in pain.

"You see," he crouches before me, "it's called culling the herd. Too many hybrids were created. There were never supposed to be that many."

"I know what you did. Your military labs created the hybrids. You tricked them. Gave them false memories. Why?"

His face darkens. "How did you find out?" He rises and shakes his head. "Doesn't matter. The hybrids once served a purpose. Now they don't. I played a hand in creating them. Now I end them." He approaches a console. "With this..." He pounds his fingers on a digital screen. A hologram projects a 3-D view of an arsenal of drones. They hover in the sky above Section H, loitering with their grenade-like warheads.

Tyren shakes his head. "Don't do this, Will."

"Too late. It's already set in motion." Hunter rubs his hands together. "We needed to rebuild that part of town, anyway."

"You can't control the blast zones." I climb unsteadily to my feet. "You'll end up killing innocent citizens! Women, *children*. Paul might not make it."

"I'm cleaning Spark City up. Like I said, the hybrids don't serve a purpose any more. Paul's on his own."

"What purpose *did* they serve?" He hasn't set the detonator sequence yet. If I can keep him talking…

Hunter rocks back on his heels. He picks up the helmet again after nodding to the soldiers. "The chair."

Murphy and the other male soldier grab me, remove my handcuffs, and haul me into a vertically inclined chair off to the side of the room. They strap me in, and I'm surrounded by tubes and medical instruments like I saw in my visions. The instruments are the ones used on Gatz was on when they spliced his DNA and performed their terrible experiments.

The woman hooks up a long, probing needle deep into a vein on my uninjured arm. I cry out in pain, feeling dizzy. My vision clouds, but I push my mangled hand into the seat so the pain keeps me alert. My blood seeps through a long tube into a machine. "What is this?"

Hunter approaches with a grin. "It will all make sense soon."

Vance, help me. What can I do? I think.

Vance saunters over and leans against a nearby wall. *Let's hear what he has to say, shall we?* he says.

"Many years ago," Hunter says, "I was a lowly private, given nothing but grunt work. My superiors didn't see my potential. They didn't guess my genius. But then one day, an opportunity came up to work at a medical research facility. My bunkmate got the assignment. I congratulated him, but I seethed inside. I couldn't believe I'd been passed over. My jealousy ate me up, so I threw him off the roof, made it look accidental, and took the assignment myself."

Out of the corner of my eye, I see Tyren struggle against his handcuffs, but Murphy steps in and points a rifle at him.

"I climbed the ladder quickly at the med lab. The Super Soldier project was my idea." He gazes up as if lost in the past. "My masterpiece."

"Super Soldier project?" I ask.

"The Heavies were strong, their weaponry advanced. As our outfit joined forces with European militaries, we knew it was a losing battle. The Middle East—where the Heavies launched their invasion—suffered the most, losing tens of millions of civilian lives. The military forces fought, but were decimated. Scattered. I pitched the idea of super soldiers—an army that could fight the alien invaders. Foreign invaders against creatures with superhuman strength. I became fast friends with a scientist. Kenmore could solve any problem. He was absolutely brilliant." Hunter gestures at the machines I'm hooked up to. "He invented this technology and perfected gene recombination. DNA splicing. He made the impossible come true."

Murphy and the two soldiers exchange bewildered glances. They're hearing this for the first time, too. How long has Hunter kept the hybrid origins a secret?

I peek sideways at Tyren. Hunter catches me, and his gaze darts wildly between us.

"Looking to your precious Tyren for reassurance? Don't be fooled by his dreamy, fatherly wisdom act. He knew all about the Super Soldier program. He was part of it from the beginning." Hunter saunters over to Tyren, who hangs his head low. "Isn't that right, Tyren? After all, it was you who brought Ida to me."

My heart jumps into my throat. A lying couple took me from Woodlawn Youth Improvement Center and took me to the lab. Not Tyren.

Against the wall, Vance chuckles. *Oh, this is getting good. I think I like Hunter.*

"You see, Ida..." Hunter fixates on me. "The Super Soldier project wasn't given enough time. Some soft-hearted politician grew a conscience and ordered a halt on all hybrid experiments. The idiot." He paces. "We'd only reached stage two. We still had two more stages to go. The animal creatures were strong, yes, but we hadn't yet been able to program their hostility and anger. That would only come with more surgery and splicing, but the program was canceled. It was short-sighted. A mistake."

I sneak a glance at Tyren, and our eyes connect.

The tube with my blood continues draining, making me weak and foggy.

Hunter goes on. "But Kenmore and I made a pact. We continued our experiments in secret. We brought in Tyren because we needed a third to carry out our plans. The top brass had taken away our access to animal DNA, so we did what we could with leftover samples and Kenmore…improvised." Hunter leans in close. "Our access to volunteer soldiers cut off. We were forced to experiment on human subjects."

"You mean experiment on children. We were orphaned, homeless, and brought there against our wills. I was only seventeen."

He leans back. "Your precious Tyren brought you to me. Offered you up. You were one of the early subjects."

"How many of us were there?" I want to keep him going. If I survive this, I swear I'll burn that lab to the ground with every scientist in it.

"You were patient three," Hunter says. "There were at least twenty of you, I can't quite recall. Can you, Tyren?"

Tyren grunts and shuffles his feet. The soldiers stand by with their weapons.

"Tyren's being a grump. He never enjoyed this as much as me." Hunter paces in a circle. "Well, patients one and two were abysmal failures. Things went so haywire, they both committed suicide in their rooms. Pity."

My head lolls to the side and my vision blurs.

"That's enough," Hunter says to the female

soldier, who then withdraws the long needle from my arm.

I inhale deeply and try to focus.

"Then you came along. And your results were… well, unexpected. We designed you to be a fighter. Strong, lighting-fast reflexes, strategic. But something happened. Rather than the killer instinct we thought we'd infused into you, you ended up as a healer." He eyes Tyren. "Interesting results, but not a super soldier who could mow down fifty Heavies at a time."

Despite my haze, I glance at the flashing digital screen on the console. Hunter still hasn't started the countdown.

"I wanted to dispose of you," Hunter says. "Write you off as another failure, but Tyren intervened on your behalf."

Across the room, Tyren lifts his head.

"Tyren was assigned to active duty—leading a platoon. He said he'd take you and monitor you as long as we wiped your memory of the surgeries and experiments. As long as we wiped the memory of him and what he did to you."

"Enough," Tyren shouts. "Let her go. She's done nothing wrong. Only a pawn in your game. Let her go, and you and I can finish this. Hand to hand."

Hunter grins. "Temper, temper. Always spoiling for a fight, my man. Now that you two are reunited, I plan to study Ida's power. Has it changed over the years, I wonder?" He waves at Tyren. "Put him in the hot seat."

Murphy and the other grunt grab Tyren and buckle him into another chair like mine. The woman injects another needle deep into his veins.

"No!" I twist in my chair, trying to stop them. If my touch killed the woman soldier, what will my blood do to Tyren?

"Why?" Hunter strides over. "What's the matter? Your blood should strengthen him."

"He could die," I say.

Hunter narrows his eyes. "What do you mean?"

"Something, my coma maybe…changed me. I can't heal anymore." I stare down, avoiding his eyes boring into me.

"I suspected something was wrong. A drone filmed part of the riot. The footage showed you attempting to heal the soldier, but she died. I thought her injuries must have been severe. But you…" He leans closer.

"You killed her," he says.

Chapter 36
Inject

Hunter's body trembles as he howls with laughter. "Your touch *kills* now." He clutches his stomach. "Oh, perfect," he says, wiping away tears. "I couldn't have planned this any better."

My eyelids grow heavy.

"Give her something to pep her up." He motions to the woman. "I want her alert when I annihilate Section H."

The nurse eyes me as she hooks an IV bag on a stand, then inserts another needle into my forearm. "This'll help you regain a bit of strength," she says under her breath.

"What do you think changed you?" Hunter scratches his head. "We've known all along you have the alien steel inside you. Then you were in a coma. Something must have changed the nanobots in your blood." He searches my face for a reaction.

I try to mask my emotions, so he won't have the satisfaction of figuring me out.

"Well, it doesn't matter." He shakes his head. "I have your DNA and your warped nanotech. I'll create an army of soldiers that can kill with their touch."

My head's clearing. "I'll kill you and hunt down everyone in those labs." I want to rip myself out of the restraints and tear him to pieces.

"Yeah? You want to kill me and destroy your sample?" Picking up the vial that contains my blood, Hunter approaches a console and slides it into a slot. A digital screen flashes on and starts a rapid analysis. "If I let you out of those restraints, would you fight me for the sample?"

I strain against the cuffs. My damaged hand throbs with a dull pain.

He leans in, his face inches from mine. "It's too late. The analyzer is already transmitting the composite of your blood and DNA to the lab. They have it already." His eyes shine.

My stomach sinks. How many people will die as they conduct their horrific experiments?

"You should thank me. You have an extraordinary gift. Your DNA may be the key to defeating the Heavies."

"How many innocent lives will you destroy in the process?" I ask.

"A few. You've got me there." He saunters across the room. "But their deaths will advance science and help save us all."

On the inverted table, Tyren clenches his hands into tight fists. The soldiers keep their gazes locked on Hunter.

"Let's do our first test, shall we?" Hunter removes the vial from the analyzer. "Needle."

The medic quickly retrieves a fresh needle wrapped in a plastic bag and passes it to Hunter. He draws some of my blood before snapping the vial back into the machine.

A chill runs down my spine and legs as I follow Hunter's stare. "No, please!"

Hunter walks toward Tyren. "We've been through so much, man. You were a good partner," Hunter says. "But now, you're on her side. And that won't fly."

Tyren tenses, and his muscles are rigid.

"I need a test," Hunter says. "No hard feelings, huh?"

"Hunter, don't do this." I fight against the buckles strapping me to the chair. My legs flail as I kick them, trying to gain leverage. The heavy seat slides back a few inches.

"Any last words?" Hunter leans in close to Tyren.

"Ida, I'm sorry I lied to you," Tyren says. "I'm sorry I ever hurt you. I love you like a daughter. Be strong."

Hunter drives the needle into Tyren's arm and pushes my blood into his veins.

"Tyren!" I shout. He swallows and looks up as if in prayer.

Hunter checks his biocuff. "Computer, make a record. Subject Reginald Tyren injected at 2107 hours. Pending reaction."

Then Tyren twitches and shakes all over, his muscles bulging against the straps.

"Computer, subject is experiencing sudden, severe tremors, and I observed a blue light surging across his skin. Most interesting results."

Tyren opens his eyes and locks his gaze on me.

"I'm sorry," I say as tears stream down my face.

Then he seizes up. His body goes limp.

Hunter strides over to the console and triggers the drones. The clock counts down.

Fifteen minutes.

Chapter 37
Control

"You bastard! You promised an hour." My heart feels like it's wedged in my throat. I can't believe Tyren is dead, and Section H is about to be annihilated.

Hunter shrugs. "Life isn't fair. The more hybrids destroyed, the better. They should be grateful I gave them any warning at all."

As seconds tick by, it feels as though I'm running against a tidal wave. "Hunter, please. Stop the bombing. What will this solve? You'll end up killing innocent humans, too. Everyone will turn against you." What can I say to change this madman's mind?

"Hmm. A few civilian casualties are to be expected. I'll blame the hybrids. Say they took hostages."

I look at Murphy and the two soldiers. "Do you see what he's doing? He's going to destroy Section H and everyone in it. There are innocent people there. Not to mention thousands of hybrid lives that'll be wiped out in an instant."

Murphy stares with a frown. The other two avert their eyes.

"Murphy," I shout. "Are you listening?"

"I'm obeying orders. The Colonel knows best," he says.

Hunter folds his arms across his chest. "It's useless, Ida. My troops won't disobey me. Save your breath."

What can I do? Tyren is dead. My body shakes as time slips away.

"Thirteen minutes until detonation," announces a flat AI voice.

Vance lurks in the corners of the room.

Inside my mind, I beg. *Vance, help me. Do something.*

I'm out of ideas, he says. *You're on your own. He's going to blow the hybrids up, and there's nothing you can do to stop it.*

If there's one thing Hunter has loads of, it's pride, along with a heaping dose of arrogance. Will he rise to a challenge? He busies himself at the command console, his back to me.

"Fight me like a soldier, Hunter." My voice is firm.

He pauses. "What did you say?"

"Let me out of these chains and fight me. Hand to hand combat. No weapons. Just you and me."

He laughs. "You'd destroy me with your touch. I'm no idiot."

He attends to the machine, but I want him to take the bait.

Vance leans against a wall, studying his nails.

"I have an idea." Hunter crosses the room to the bench near his soldiers and picks up the steel helmet. "I wear this, and the fight is fair. You against armor. Are you in?"

Careful, Vance warns.

"In."

That helmet is more powerful than anything you've experienced, Vance says.

"I'll take my chances," I say out loud.

"Have it your way. Open room," Hunter says, and the immense glass dome structure enclosing the command center slides away to reveal the night sky. A balmy, frenzied wind swirls around us. The consoles and stations shift neatly into corners, leaving a generous space for our combat.

Then he pulls the helmet on. Nothing happens.

I eye Vance.

He needs to activate the helmet first, Vance says. *Does he know?*

Hunter approaches a console and places his palm on a biometric screen. In the middle of the room, a floor panel slides open. A platform appears and rises from below. A thick metal rod rests on the center.

"While Gatz and his hybrid friends were scratching their heads over how this thing worked, I was busy tearing these towers apart, looking for any clue how the helmet worked. Imagine my surprise when I found schematics hidden in a vault."

Ah, he found the vault, Vance says. *I'd been wondering about that.*

"All I needed was to get back the stolen helmet. I

couldn't blow up Section H until I had it." Hunter approaches the rod and grabs it in both hands. "Luckily, you arrived and handed it to me. You know how much trouble you saved me?"

A jolt of current travels from his arms, across his chest and neck until it reaches his head. The electricity shocks the headgear, and Hunter pulls away from the activation device.

The helmet vibrates and seems to come alive on its own. Layers of shimmering metallic steel unfold and wrap across Hunter's torso and midsection before enclosing his arms and legs.

Now Hunter wears a fully adaptive metal suit perfectly aligned to his body. Somehow, the metal flexes and melds with his limbs; the advanced tech makes the best armor of our marines look like a tin can.

Marvelous, Vance purrs.

Hunter holds up his arms and admires his new cyber armor. He spins around and jumps, testing the weight of the suit.

My prototype. It's magnificent, Vance says.

I'm running out of time. "Let me out," I say.

"Murphy, release her," Hunter barks.

The soldier jogs over and releases the buckles holding me in. I slide off the table and fall to my knees. My legs feel rubbery. I lean on the edge of the table to pull myself up, shake my legs until the feeling in them returns.

"Eleven minutes until detonation," the AI says.

I scan the room for a weapon, anything I can use

in defense. Against the wall, I spy large steel pipes. I lunge forward and pull on a long piece with my right hand. Yanking it with all my weight, the metal bends slowly. Groaning, I kick and pull until the force snaps it out of its joint. The pipe clatters to the floor, and I grab it, feeling the cold steel in my grip. I advance on Hunter as he explores the mech suit.

He levitates a foot off the floor, testing the hover ability when I ram the steel pipe into his back like a sword. He lurches forward and staggers, but doesn't fall.

Rounding on me swiftly, he sulks. "That wasn't nice." He advances, propelled by the suit, hands outstretched, reaching for me.

I dodge to the right. His metallic fingers graze my shoulder. Spinning, I whip the steel rod toward him. The metal careens off the armored suit without making a dent.

Useless. I'm a gnat fighting a bear. "Vance, how do I fight the suit?" I'm beyond caring if anyone hears me talking to Vance.

You can't. Vance circles the edges of the room like a referee in a boxing match.

Hunter spins and hovers several feet off the ground, then surges forward, launching his body at me. This time, he grabs my arm and drags me through the air. I land against the wall. My back screams in pain as he knocks the wind from me.

He flies to the center of the room. "I'll be unstoppable. An army of soldiers who can kill with their touch and me leading the charge." He catches his reflection in the glass panes. "I'll send the Heavies scurrying back to whatever cold rock they came from. Then I'll conquer every country on Earth. No army can stop me."

As Murphy and the soldiers gaze at the suit, distracted, I grab a pulse rifle leaning against a wall. "Think again, Hunter." I lunge forward, firing rounds at him.

He flails, his body crashing against a window partition. Shards of broken glass spray onto the open-air deck where he falls. Motionless.

I jog over and kick him. Then he grabs my ankle and bursts up into the air. He drags me as he levitates, and I'm hanging upside down as he cackles.

"Vance, help me!"

Hunter tosses me onto the deck like a wet rag. My shoulder hits the concrete first, sending daggers of pain into my arm and shot-up hand. I slide across the surface and my head and neck hit the small waist-high wall that separates me from a sixty-five-story plunge.

My vision fades. Then silence. Hunter and the mech suit disappear. The soldiers have vanished. Tyren's dead body erased. It's just me and Vance on the rooftop.

"Like old times." Vance looms above me.

"No time." I crawl forward at his feet, staring up. "Tell me how to beat the suit. Gatz, Lucy, everyone will die."

Vance crouches and faces me at eye-level. "Let me

take over your body. I know a weak spot in the armor."

"Is this a trick?" I can't possibly trust him.

"You want to win?" he asks. "The clock is ticking."

Alkina warned me never to give up control to Vance. But what choice do I have? I'll do anything to stop Hunter.

"Promise me…" I grab his collar. "Win and stop the bombing. Do you swear?"

His red pupils shine amid the steel blue of his eyes. "I promise."

I squeeze my eyes shut and regain consciousness. Hunter zooms around the rooftop, picks up a heavy metal chair, and flings it at me. I scamper out of the way as the chair bounces up and over the ledge.

A cacophony of sirens erupts from the streets below, followed by the sound of gunfire echoing through the canyons of skyscrapers that surround us. I assume it's Gatz and other hybrids leading an assault.

Hunter peers over the edge, then aims an arm at the street below. "Fire ballistic." A missile ejects from the suit.

I grab another of the large chairs and leap at him. The chair acts as a battering ram and he's trapped in the legs. I pin him to the ledge, his back leaning over.

But he bursts forward and bats me with his arm. I gasp for air as my chest is struck with what feels like a truck. Then I black out. When I come to, I'm lying on concrete, clouds swirling in the night sky overhead reflecting the neon lights of the city.

Metal footsteps bear down, and suddenly Hunter's metal fist screams toward my face. I roll to the side. The cement cracks beneath his fist.

"Vance, now," I say. My body courses with a frenzied tingling. I raise my head, cry out, and a blue light energy fills me.

I give up control.

Chapter 38
Destiny

"Six minutes until detonation," the AI says.

Vance gazes down at my hands. I'm a spectator in my body with him in the driver's seat. I see through his eyes, experience the same smells, and endure his pain. Is this what he felt like trapped inside me?

Hunter lunges toward me and lands a punch on my right shoulder that sends us staggering.

Rage boils up inside, and Vance clenches my fists. He sprints toward Hunter, catching him off-guard from behind. Vance scrambles onto Hunter's back, straddles the armored suit, and grips his neck.

Hunter tries to grab my body with both arms, but the suit isn't designed to reach around.

Vance rips off a panel on the suit's back, just below the neck, exposing a circuit board. Hunter roars and surges backward, ramming into a wall.

A cry leaps from my throat as Vance loses his grip around the metal hulk's neck. My body slumps to the ground.

Vance, I call out. He's not answering, and I feel trapped. A hideous claustrophobia.

"Four minutes until detonation," the AI reminds us.

This can't be happening. In minutes, those I love will be reduced to rubble.

Hunter stomps in his steel suit. Laughter sounds from behind the helmet. "You thought you had me."

He lifts me under my arms and hoists me up. My head lolls to the side because Vance is still passed out.

I scream inside my head, *Wake up, Vance*. I want to climb out of this cell I'm trapped in and fight Hunter myself. Damn it. Why did I give up control?

Hunter strides to the ledge and hovers, holding my body over the street below. From above, it appears the androids and Scramblers have been disabled, or at least subdued. Gatz must have used the deprogramming command. The hybrids are barricaded behind a concrete wall, and there's still a standoff with the human soldiers.

"Three minutes until detonation," the AI says.

Vance stirs. Finally. He comes to and screams when he realizes my body hangs in the air.

"Your friends think they've won," Hunter says. "But it won't matter when they learn what I'm capable of now."

Vance, do something, I beg.

"I can't," Vance answers.

Hunter goes on. "My soldiers will grow even stronger after seeing me crush the hybrids."

"Two minutes," the AI says.

I can't let this happen. *Vance, I'm taking control again*, I tell him.

Hunter brings my face close to his. "I'll fix whatever you've done to my androids, and I'll execute every hybrid I can find for treason."

I squeeze my eyes shut and conjure the image of the yellow flower. Alkina. I see my blood pumping through Tyren, killing him. Memories, sensations, my encounters with Vance flood me. Gatz's voice in my ears, saying "I love you."

"How would you like to take the express elevator down to your friends?" Hunter says.

A pulsating energy erupts inside me. My body trembles, then shakes with violence.

Inside the mech suit, Hunter's eyes widen.

Blue energy envelops me. Vance thrashes inside me again. Then he's gone. Vanished.

Night wind rushes around me. I'm inside my body again, fully aware I'm about to fall to a gruesome death. At the mercy of a madman.

I calm my body and stare into Hunter's eyes. "Rassvet," I say.

The cyber mech suit twitches. A high-pitched whirring noise sounds an alert. Digital computations flash across the armor's visor. Inside, Hunter scowls.

Then the suit maneuvers onto the deck, descending. It places me down gently.

Inside, Hunter screams and struggles to control the suit, but the mech strides toward a glass pane, studying its reflection. It places a hand on the glass. Does it know what it is? That it nearly killed me?

The suit spins around and ejects Hunter. He crumples to the ground and covers his head, cowering before the suit.

I grab a rifle and aim at Hunter as the elevator door flies open. Gatz, Paul, and Lucy rush in. They subdue Murphy and the soldiers, then watch in awe as Vance's cyber suit neatly folds itself up, becoming a helmet resting on the floor.

The AI interrupts. "One minute until detonation."

"Cover Hunter!" I yell as I sprint to the command console. I study the screen and find a disable command, then punch it.

The clock keeps going. "Forty-eight seconds."

"Gatz! I need help." My hands shake and adrenaline floods me.

The AI says, "Biometric identification required to disable detonation."

"Get Hunter," I shout.

Gatz and Paul lift him by the shoulders and drag him to the console. Paul yanks Hunter's hand up and thrusts his palm onto the screen.

Hunter thrashes in their grip. "This is how you repay family? With betrayal," he tells Paul.

"You're not my family," Paul says.

"Thirty seconds until detonation," the AI says.

"It's not working," Paul cries out. "Uncle Will, why won't it stop?"

The Colonel presses his lips tight. Paul shoves him against the console and this time presses on top of Hunter's hand.

But the timer sounds a twenty-second warning.

"Ida! Gatz, do something," Lucy yells.

Paul releases Hunter and backs away, shuddering. The Colonel falls to the floor on his knees.

Gatz leaps onto Hunter, brandishing his massive claws as he grips the man's throat. "Tell me," he snarls, "how to turn these goddamn bombs off."

The sharp edges draw tiny beads of blood from Will's neck. With huge eyes, he stammers, "P-password."

"Tell me." Gatz growls, leaning into Hunter's crazed face.

"Vance Drem," Hunter says.

Paul grips the edges of the console. "Vance Drem," he speaks into the screen.

"Password accepted," the screen reads. A few seconds pass and I hold my breath. "Detonation averted," the computer AI chirps.

We erupt into cheers. Lucy jumps into the air and screams. "We did it!"

Gatz shouts into his comms. "Pilar, you there? We disarmed it. The drones are disarmed and returning to HQ. Section H is safe. I repeat, Section H is safe."

I fall to my knees in relief. We came so close. Hunter nearly destroyed the hybrids.

Paul kicks his uncle on the ground. The large man's body flails, and his eyes dart around, searching for his soldiers. Paul grabs Hunter's collar and hits him in the jaw with a mean hook. "Monster. You nearly killed us all!" Then he spits on him as Hunter crawls away on his knees, shielding his head from more blows.

Gatz places an arm on Paul's chest. "Enough. We'll make sure he gets justice."

While catching my breath, I search my mind for any trace of Vance. He seems to have vanished, but is he really gone? He's been a part of me for so long, I can't remember what it felt like without him haunting my every thought.

A vision comes to me. A military tribunal convenes. Hunter wears a black suit. The court announces its ruling…*innocent*.

But how? A technicality?

My pulse surges and my adrenaline spikes. I race forward and scoop up the cyber helmet, pulling it down over my head. The metal slides over me, folds in and around the contours of my body like a wetsuit. And then I'm flying as I leap across the room and shove Gatz to the side.

"Hey—" he yells. Lucy and Paul duck for cover.

I grab Hunter up and off the ground. He weighs practically nothing with the powered suit. I fly to the edge and land on the railing. I dangle Hunter over the street below. City lights sparkle all around him.

He grabs onto my arm. "Please!" His red-rimmed eyes plead with me while his legs flail.

Behind me, I hear the others.

"Ida, what are you doing?" Panic in Gatz's voice.

"He won't get a fair trial." My computer-generated voice sounds hollow. Distant. "He'll get away with it."

"No," Gatz argues. "We'll see that the trial is fair,. No tricks. No military interference."

"He murdered Tyren," I say.

"And countless others. He'll rot in jail," Gatz says. I want to believe him, but if my vision proves to be true, all of this is for nothing.

"He deserves to die." I loosen my grip somewhat. His jacket slips further through my steel hands. Hunter twists and struggles, glimpsing down in horror.

I enjoy his torture. Revel in it. Is this what I am? Has Vance changed me into a murderous monster?

"Ida." Lucy's voice breaks my concentration. She's close behind me. "Ida, listen to me. Remember what you told me at the pond that day?"

Hunter's jacket rips. He's holding onto my robot wrist now.

"You said you'd stop using your nanotech if it hurt people," Lucy says. "Vance tried to corrupt you. But you're still you."

Hunter's grip weakens. He slips and hangs by one hand now, flailing, his eyes bulging.

"You're not a killer, Ida," Gatz says.

I'm not Vance. Yet the urge to murder Hunter consumes me. Not in front of Lucy. She's the only thing stopping me from dropping him to his death. Her shock—her inevitable sadness—will be more than I can bear. I'll seek my vengeance another time. Soon.

I swing my other arm out and catch Hunter by the wrist as he loses his grasp. Dragging him up, I toss him on to the rooftop where he crumples.

Hovering five feet above, I gaze down at Gatz,

Lucy, and Paul. I'm different from them. I'll never be normal, content, or happy.

Changed forever in a lab, I was meant to be a weapon. But the scientists failed the first time. Now they have what they wanted. I'm a weapon. A killer.

Now I know my destiny. I'll serve justice to the scientists by killing them with my deadly touch. The touch *they* gave me.

I soar into the night sky until my friends become a speck in the distance.

Chapter 39
Journey

Lucy marches onto a raised platform in front of the assembled group of thirty young soldiers. Bright sun illuminates flecks of gold in her long, braided hair. I've never seen her this way; she looks intense, authoritative. I'm impressed.

The troops are a mix of human and hybrid new recruits, many of whom witnessed Colonel Hunter's authoritative regime and are eager to make a fresh start.

She addresses the group. "Our first lesson is how to stand when you're preparing for hand-to-hand combat."

I observe from a distance as Lucy delivers one of the first lessons I taught her during our fight lessons. What feels like ages ago was just a few years. Before everything that happened with Vance, my coma, and then Hunter.

I want to watch longer, but I have a meeting. I journey into the Marine Command Center, now located on the second floor with a great open view of the Spark City river.

In the lobby, a variety of species—hybrids, androids, men and women—work together to rebuild the damage done by Hunter one month ago. As they patch walls and paint, the place feels alive, full of activity and energy. The city will be stronger.

I skip the elevator and take the stairs two at a time. On the second floor, I enter a massive command center room that looks like the bridge of a starship.

Paul presides at the head of a long table. He's clean shaven and appears years older than nineteen. One of the youngest commanders in the history of the marines, Paul makes a striking leader. He offered me a promotion to major, but I refused. I want no part of the military.

I salute him. "Sir."

"Ida." He smiles. "Today's the day?"

I nod. "My bike?"

"As you requested, it's outside, parked on the street ready for you to load up. So is the other bike."

"Good, thanks." I rock back on my heels, not sure what else to say.

"You sure you want to do this?" he asks.

"Positive."

"Well, I'd rather have you stay here and help me lead, but I understand…"

I shove my hands in my pocket, not wanting to have this conversation again.

"Off the record, if there's still a chance you'd want

to stay in Spark City, or come back and serve again in the Marines, just say the word."

"Paul, we've been over this. Trust me, I've gone through it a million times in my head. Finding the labs and destroying my DNA is the only way I can make sure…" I swallow. "Make sure I don't hurt people."

He studies my expression, then lowers his eyes. "You said your farewell to Lucy and Vera?"

"Yes." I know his next question.

"What about Gatz?"

I glance away. "What about him? There's nothing to say."

"He's come to me several times and sent messages." Paul comes closer, forcing me to meet his gaze. "He doesn't understand why you don't want to see him."

"Leaving's hard enough, Paul. I don't want to make things worse. It's better if I just leave."

"So, that's it? You won't meet with him. No message? At least tell him goodbye?" Paul asks.

"No."

"I hope you don't regret it," he says.

"You'll make a good commander, Paul. What you went through with your uncle… Most soldiers never face that kind of test in their lifetime."

"Yeah. I wish I'd stood up to him earlier. I hope he enjoys rotting in his prison cell."

"On another topic, where are you taking Lucy on your first date?" I ask.

He puts an arm around my shoulders and walks

with me. "So, I was thinking a romantic picnic at the museum next to the Tyrannosaurus Rex skeleton."

"Wow, you sure know how to make a girl swoon. Good luck with that." I give him a soft punch on his arm. "I'm sure she'll love it. She's weird like that."

He laughs and blushes.

"I hate goodbyes, so I'm out of here." I turn to leave.

He pats my arm. "Be careful, Ida. I expect frequent updates. If you need backup…"

"Hey, I've got my trusty sidekicks, remember? They're all the backup I'll need." I give him a final salute before I leave.

After retrieving my backpack, I walk past Lucy's initiation class again. She tosses me a glance. I wave, and she winks. We've said our goodbyes. She was stronger than I thought she'd be.

In the last few weeks, she's grown up a lot. She understands why I'm leaving, and best of all, she accepts why I don't want to talk to Gatz. Only she knows how much it hurt to have Vance inside me, knowing I couldn't control him.

She's seen Gatz nearly every day and gives me a report. He's been reinstated as mayor of Spark City. An election will follow in a year, but for now, he's savoring his role as leader again. After Hunter's defeat, martial law was revoked, and the hybrids were set free to move about the city.

The entirety of Vance's androids were given the de-programming command, freeing them from their destructive coding, and the city council elected to bestow on them a set of rights protecting them as a new class of citizens. In exchange, they agreed to abide by a law to never hurt humans or hybrids.

Most humans have fled the city. Too many rights given to those who are different. Hunter's brainwashing went deep, and some of it may never be undone. The city has peace for now.

But I won't have peace until I find the medical lab where scientists held me captive. Where they created hybrids. I'm leaving Spark City and traveling across the country for the desert, but I won't be alone.

The doctors who tortured me and countless others will pay. I'll hunt them down one by one if I have to.

So, I'm finally leaving Spark City like I'd originally planned. I just wish it didn't hurt so much.

I couldn't bring myself to see Gatz after the night on the roof. He'd witnessed me at my lowest. In a rage, I nearly killed Hunter. It wasn't Vance acting. It was me.

Hunter deserved to die. I only stopped because of what Lucy said. The scientists I'm hunting deserve to die.

Gatz and Lucy think I'm not a killer, but they're wrong.

And Vance? Gone for now, but he's somewhere inside me, buried deep. Locked away. I practice mind training three times a day now. Paul told me about a brilliant psychologist in Arizona who specializes in tough cases. Maybe I'll pay him a visit.

Vance changed me forever. I'll never touch someone with bare hands again.

I still have a functioning left hand. When Hunter shot off three fingers, I opted not to have a prosthesis. Paul and Lucy tried to convince me it would be state-of-the-art with no side effects. But after my experience with Vance, I couldn't bear to have metal fingers like his. I'll make do.

It hurts to leave Gatz without saying goodbye. I love him, but I can't touch him. What's the point of loving someone you can't ever be with?

Better for everyone if I get the hell out of Spark City. I'll never be normal or carefree. Not when my mission is to bring justice to the men behind the labs.

I find my bike parked exactly where Paul said it would be. Securing my pack, I take one last glimpse up at the tall circular towers and savor a farewell view of the river.

I hear a roar as another motorcycle kick-starts. Ogre rolls out of the shadows of the garage and pulls up. A box strapped behind his seat contains the mech helmet.

The robot salutes, his steel arm glistening in the sun. "Greetings, Ida. Ready to cruise? Put the pedal to the metal?"

I toss my motorcycle helmet on. "Hey, Ogre. Can you tone it down a notch? The lingo programming that Lucy gave you is getting on my last nerve."

"No problemo." He gives an okay sign with one of his steel hands.

I roll my eyes but can't stop a chuckle.

As I start my bike, the engine comes alive in a familiar hum, soothing my nerves. The roar of the engine grows louder. I close my eyes and inhale deeply, relishing the open road ahead of me.

And the chance to take care of unfinished business.

I open my eyes. "Kenmore," I say, my voice low. "I'm coming for you."

Something stirs inside me.

Ogre and I and speed away, leaving the city behind.

Dear Reader,

Thank you for reading Dormant! Are you ready to find out what's next for Ida and her robot sidekick, Ogre?

Book 4 is called *SALVAGE*, and it's full of twists and turns that'll have you guessing.

Ida's on the hunt for the scientist who tortured her and changed her life forever. She travels to the desert in search of answers. And justice.

But, something's wrong. Very wrong. Will the secrets of the past spell death for humankind?

Find it here: https://geni.us/salvagebook

Cameron Coral

P.S. - Did you enjoy this book? I'd love a review wherever you purchased this book if you have a few minutes. Reviews mean a lot to me. They show me you want me to keep writing, and they help other readers discover my books. Thank you kindly!

Also by Cameron Coral

Rusted Wasteland Series:

STEEL GUARDIAN

STEEL DEFENDER

STEEL PROTECTOR

STEEL SIEGE

STEEL SOLDIER

STEEL LEGACY

STEEL APOCALYPSE (A Robot's Journal) - free on
cameroncoral.com/blockjournal

Cyborg Guardian Chronicles:

STOLEN FUTURE

CODED RED

ORIGIN LOOP

Rogue Spark Series:

ALTERED

BRINK

DORMANT

SALVAGE

AFTER WE FALL (A Rogue Spark Novel) - free on
CameronCoral.com

Short Stories:

CROSSING THE VOID: A Space Opera Science-Fiction Short Story

About the Author

Cameron Coral is an award-nominated science fiction author. Her book *Steel Guardian* about a post-apocalyptic CleanerBot placed second in the Self-Published Science Fiction Competition (SPSFC).

Growing up with a NASA engineer in the family instilled a deep respect for science and for asking lots of questions. Watching tons of Star Trek episodes helped, too. Her imagination is fueled by breakthroughs in robotics, space travel, and psychology.

After moving around a lot (Canada, Arizona, Maryland, Australia), she now lives in northern Illinois with her husband and a "shorty" Jack Russell terrier who runs the house.

Want a free novel, advance copies of books, and occasional rants about why robots are awesome? Visit her website: CameronCoral.com

facebook.com/cameroncoralauthor

instagram.com/cameroncoralauthor

tiktok.com/@cameroncoral

Acknowledgments

I owe a debt of gratitude to you, dear reader, for taking a chance and picking up this book. I hope these pages transported you to another world for a bit and that you enjoyed the ride.

Ida Sarek is a character who's been bouncing around in my head for many years. She's an amalgamation of all the strong, ass-kicking sci-fi heroines I love: Ripley, Kara Thrace, Molly Millions, Katniss Everdeen, Leia, Jessica Jones, Sarah Connor, Trinity, Dana Scully, and many more I'm forgetting.

I'm not sure where the idea to have a character who can heal came from exactly. I guess in some ways, it's a superpower I'd like to have. While not as popular as flying or being invisible, being able to bring someone back to life would be incredible—and dangerous if the power fell into the wrong hands. Can you imagine certain dictators from the past or present having someone like Ida to keep reviving them?

I imagine someone like Ida would make the ultimate bodyguard.

Thank you to my ever-patient and supportive husband, Steve, for being my alpha-reader, idea bouncer-offer, and for making me breakfast many mornings.

Thanks to Mom for shuttling me to the library so much when I was a kid and not intervening when I started bringing home *Dracula*, Stephen King books, and other creepy stories when I was a kid. And also, for letting me watch *V, Twilight Zone, Star Trek, Manimal, Monsters*, and all the cool 80s sci-fi shows I wanted. Thanks for being a real-life ass-kicking heroine.

Thanks to Dad and Sherry for encouraging me to write and pursue my creativity. You both taught me it's okay to follow the beat of my own drum, be silly, and have more fun in life.

Thank you to my amazing, supportive friends and extended family! Finally, I can share my books with you! I can't possibly list everyone here because I am blessed to have a "framily" that is beyond compare.

I dedicate this series to my stepdad, Mike Roberto, who passed away in 2014. One Christmas, he gave me a gift that changed everything—*Salem's Lot* by Stephen King. Wow, did I love that book when I was eight. I didn't understand everything I read, but the tiny spark of an idea flowered: *I want to be a writer someday.*

If you enjoyed DORMANT and would like to hear more from me, I extend a warm welcome to join my email newsletter. It takes a minute to sign up. Just visit CameronCoral.com and you'll find a sign-up button. You'll also get a free story!

I send 1-2 emails per month about fun stuff—pictures, videos, and personal updates. Often, I share updates about what I'm writing, short stories, or rants about why robots are awesome. You'll see cosplay pics from when I attend comic conventions and meet my dog, Marty.

I take your email privacy seriously, and I have a detailed privacy policy on my website. You can unsubscribe at any time. But I hope you stick around, because I have a lot to share in the years to come.

Cameron Coral

P.S. Have you ever left a review for a book you like? If you have, I promise that writer loved you for it. Reviews are how independent authors get the word out. We don't have publishers; we depend on people like you writing reviews to let other people know we're out here and you like what we do.

Also, if you have questions about the book or Ida or just want to say "hi," send me an email anytime at info@cameroncoral.com